THE
DUNWICH ROMANCE

EDWARD LEE

deadite
press

DEADITE PRESS
205 NE BRYANT
PORTLAND, OR 97211
www.DEADITEPRESS.com

AN ERASERHEAD PRESS COMPANY
www.ERASERHEADPRESS.com

ISBN: 978-1-62105-129-9

The Dunwich Romance © 2011, 2013 by Edward Lee

Cover art copyright © 2013 Jim Apalza

Printed in the USA.

Acknowledgments

Wendy Brewer, Dave Barnett, Larry Roberts, Roy Robbins; Jeff, Rose, and Carlton at Deadite; Sergeant Andrew Myers, Bob Strauss, Corie Fromkin, Thomas Bauduret, Greg James, Qwee, reelsplatter, Joey Lombardo, Scott Berke, Alex McVey, Sandy Brock and Tony, Kyle N., Sheri Gambino, Krist, Tastybabysyndrome, Travis Deputy, Shroud Magazine, Monrozombi, Zombified420, sikahtik, rhfactornl, wm ollie, Konnie, Dianna Busby; Gorch; Ashton Heyd, Bob Chaplin, Southern Blood, Hexsyn, KK, Kim, Jan, Bartek Czartoryski, Michael Preissl, Greg Hurlstone, K in D, Dancingwith2leftfeet, Dathar, eubankscs, mypaperpast, Big T, brownie, drunk yorkshireman, mastodonisgod, fizzmaster, wildwood72, airbucket, squeakytherat, ronin57, etaylor, bodydenny, demonknight80, Foxglove, Matt Parsons, Terrence Patrick Rooney, Matthew T. Carpenter, Marcie, Troy Chambers, erbroxcore, gargirl, Emperor Buyer, allnumber2, Nigel Waspfinger, Old Fan, William M. Miller, Danielle D. Smith, Lisa Clay, EdHead, Cheryl Mullenax, Bgill, jasonwulf, Frank Festa, Fred Tosi, Bigheadsballsback, and Wilum Pugmire.

For Bob Hinton,
a great fan and a great friend.

AUTHOR'S NOTE

Though a portion of H.P. Lovecraft enthusiasts are sure to curse me into the deepest pits of the Shoggoths for daring to 1) append one of the greatest horror stories ever written, and 2) for doing so in such an indelicate, microscopically sexual, and scatological manner, I suspect that a good many readers may indeed enjoy this bit of work. Moreover, I'm very grateful to those of you who are fans of my material and have continued to support these intermittent excursions into the venue of the Lovecraftian. Thank you! As a further note, for non-Lovecraftian readers, it would be much better to first read the original masterpiece, Lovecraft's *The Dunwich Horror*; and for those of you who have read it in the past—I hope you are many—treat yourself to something special and read it again. It's the type of story—like so many of the Master's—that becomes more brilliant each time you read it. It can easily be found for free at Dagonbytes and other such wonderful websites. My effort here is merely a wee, insignificant ornamentation to the ingenious original. Long live Lovecraft!

—*E.L.*

March 15, 2011

THE
DUNWICH
ROMANCE

ONE

The end of the Dunwich affair left it granted that the entirety of Wilbur Whateley's hand-written records had been directed into the possession of the renown Dr. Henry T. Armitage (A.M. Miskatonic, Ph.D. Princeton, Litt.D. Johns Hopkins, Dr.Ing. Erlangen-Nürnberg) of Miskatonic University. Dr. Armitage is due considerable credit for having broken a complex acrostic/substitution code into which these records were enciphered; and the nature of the information gleaned makes it more than reasonable that said data was never publicly released. Instead, a counterfeit explanation devised by authorities spuriously stated that the records were but gobbledygook, an account much more easily digested by all who might be interested.

To reiterate: the existence of these records is granted. What is *not* granted, however, is this: not quite all of Wilbur Whateley's records found their way to Dr. Armitage.

TWO

Sary Sladder was being molested, quite creatively, behind a briar-bordered stone fence which paralleled some unwholesome pasturage on the westerly outskirts of Dunwich, when her dismal and quite mediocre life changed forever. Though attractive in body by most local judgment, the unkempt twenty-three-year-old had long-since resigned to an existence of questionable nutrition (of which semen played a depressingly large part) and poverty so absolute it was better left undetailed. Any world-view or personal doctrine that her grey matter may have engendered will remain equally undetailed; however, it might be relevant to delegate a few words to her physical aspect: very long, tar-hued hair; curvesome in contour to a voluptuous degree, while yet hardily lean; adequately bosomed and tumescently nippled; with skin that was, as goes the cliche, alabaster-white. Lips—if anything, *overly* full—adorned a mouth bereft of front teeth thanks to a father whose explosive psychological climate was all too commonplace amongst Dunwich men; yet this misfortune reversed as Sary soon identified the act of prostitution as her only feasible mode of income-production (more than half of her engagements in this sad yet aeonian trade consisted of "oral succor," and the aforesaid missing incisors to quite a degree magnified the effectiveness of the service). All of her physical enticements, however, ended with the remainder of her visage: a mastiff attack when very young had left her minus one ear and scarred on both cheeks; she had a hopelessly collapsed nose (thanks, also, to her toper of a father); and an absolutely unvarying facial dermatological outbreak. (Less kind Dunwichers referred to her as "Stew Face.") But another disability that (like the knocked out teeth) took a turn for the better was a grievous sinus infection

13

during infancy which completely obliterated her sense of smell; hence, without ever even knowing it, Sary's destitute existence was brightened, as the groins of Dunwichers were not known for their olfactory immaculateness.

Sary at this moment found herself on the less-advantageous end of an awry business proposition. Ten cents was all she charged, yet the target of her commerce today, the burly, hare-lipped Rufus Hutchins, son of an alcoholic well-digger named Elam, made an alternative offer:

"Wal, I got ten cents, Sary, but I also got ten suthin' else."

"Ten...*what?*" Sary asked, not in reception of his meaning.

Whack! came the meaty sound of both fists slamming into her face. "Ten *knuckles,* ya dutty whore!" Rufus replied, pronouncing "whore" as "hoo-ah" in his mushy backwater dialect. He laughed and watched Sary topple to the grassy verge next to the fence. Her senses skewed; she saw proverbial stars as big sandpaper hands hauled her flannel dress up and roved her nude body. Fingertips pliered her nipples; a fist clenched her pubic thatch and *yanked,* and she yelped. "Gonna bust this hoo-ah pussy *up* with my dick, ee-yuh," assured Rufus, as the organ to which his vernacular referred had already been extracted. It dangled half-limp but when—*whack!*—he struck her once more in the head, the organ erected with an instantaneousness so thorough one would've taken it to be spring-loaded. Sary's vision smeared; she managed vocal incoherencies through the fist-induced stupor, and when she attempted to strike Rufus's contorted face, her arm only flopped about. "My pa fucked yew onct," Rufus reminded her. "Said yer cum-hole smelt wuss than a moose-gut pile ben in the woods a month," and then pushed her face to one side, exposed the unattractive aperture where her ear had been bitten off, and, for some reason knowable only to one as deranged as Rufus, expectorated liberally into that aperture. These few moments of outrage sufficed to revive some of Sary's vitality; she whipped her head back and forth as if to jettison the sputum from her ear-hole, and shrieked, "Yew're right, your daddy fucked me but his dick was so little, I didn't even *feel* it! And I also heerd yew suck *dog dick!*" Sary, in truth, had heard

14

no such thing, but felt the invention appropriate.

Rufus tensed. "Oh, so's I suck dog dick, yew say?" and then the well-digger's son brought two index fingers to his mouth, whistled quite piercingly, and called out, "Heer, Brooter! Heer, boy!" after which Sary's guts shriveled as she recalled a bit too latently that the Hutchinses owned a collie named *Brooter,* and a *vicious* collie at that.

Over the fence bounded the mangy, yellow-fanged collie, its insane eyes keen with interest. Rufus snapped his fingers, commanded, "Roll over, boy!" whereupon the animal (curiously, as if *used* to this command) circumducted itself upon the ground and spread its hind legs. Testicles large as a human's lolled in their fleshy sac, and a glistening pink tip of flesh had already begun to extrude from the penile sheath. Sary did not require notice as to what she would next be required to do.

"Thet's a *good* dutty hoo-ah, thet's a *good* Stew Face. Jess yew go on'n suck Brooter's dick...," her captor approved as Sary performed the unmentionable onus, yet with Rufus' hands about her throat, alternate options did not present themselves. In no extended time, however, the girl's skills proved sufficient to summon the bestial emission. Her first reaction was surprise—at the sheer *volume* of fluid that suddenly materialized in her oral cavity—then, the *horror* kicked in, for the taste, texture, and temperature of this aberrant discharge all combined at once, proving itself in all likelihood the most revolting substance to ever occupy space in her mouth. Her innate reflex, of course, was to expel it all as abruptly as it had appeared, yet at the same instant she would do just that, Rufus' hands tightened about her throat, and he gave every guarantee: "Yew dun't swalluh? Wal, then I'll jess have ta crush yew're head with one'a these fence-stones, then *fuck yew dead.*"

When Sary swallowed, she was impacted by the feeling of one having just been dropped into a mile-deep abysm, and as the revolting taste began to trail down to her stomach, Rufus had already pushed her on her back. "Naow we'll git'cha some cum in yew're baby-maker"—he paused on a reflection,

15

then blurted excitedly, "Ee-yuh! We'll make ya a *Rufus* baby! Then, in nine months, when it come out? I'll cut'cher tits off so's it'll starve ta death!" and as Rufus prepared to rape Sary, she unwisely pointed to the aggressor's erection, laughed, and offered, "Why, *dang,* fat-boy! Yew're dick's even littler than yer daddy's!" This, by the way, was true, and also a verisimilitude Rufus did not appreciate being reminded of.

Rufus' face went blank. "Aw, naow, Stew Face shouldn't arter've said that," and then his face bucked forward with a grimace, and he snorted fiercely, launching dual plumes of mucus out of his nostrils and into Sary's face. Sary froze in mortification, and more so when Rufus was kind enough to spread the mucus around with his big hand. Already he'd pinned her immobile to the ground via the placement of his knees into her elbows. He grabbed her head and forced it to one side, then whistled again for his mascot. "Heer, Brooter! Heer, boy!" The sated animal jumped up to tend to its master as its master had brushed aside Sary's hair in order to divulge her remaining ear.

"Sic, boy! Sic!" Rufus snarled. "Bite that ear *clean off!*"

Sary screamed as the unhinged canine surged forward with snapping jaws, and when said jaws had just begun to close over her ear, Sary screamed all the louder.

"*Eat* that ear, boy! *Gooooooooood* dawg!"

Against the ear, the jaws pulled; Sary could feel the beginnings of connective tissue tearing, even over her outraged screams. What had she done to warrant so brutal a molestation? *Gawd DANG, Gawd!* came her protestation. *I'se sorry fer bein' a whore but, holy bull-flop! What choice I got things bein' the way they is?* I.e, in spite of her horror, Sary was indignant. *Yew think mebbe Yew could have Jesus help me?*

Another few seconds were all that would be necessary for the canine to detach Sary's ear from her head, but in slightly *less* time than that...

An oddly angled shadow darkened the scene—and Brooter...released Sary's ear, yelped, and drew away, hunched down as if threatened by some awesome adversary.

"Brooter? What's wrong with yew, huh, boy?" Rufus complained. "Durn't ya wanna eat on this dutty fuck-pot's ear?" but then Rufus turned and looked up into the direction to which his animal's attention had been so abruptly diverted. At once came an eardrum-quaking—

BAM!

—so loud the sequent concussion caused the surrounding air to *thump.* The foam-mouthed canine yelped again and flipped completely around in mid-air. The unbidden somersault dropped the dog flat and dead, and half of its cranial matter had expeditiously launched from its skull.

"Why, ya done kilt my—" Rufus began to rage, but then all objections ceased when his vision acknowledged to his brain, first, an obvious firearm—a large revolver, a Webley .455, to be precise—and, second, the source of the awkward shadow.

It was a man—or some horrific *exaggeration* of a man— cumbersomely jointed as if afflicted by some disorder of the bones, the crown of whose head ran amok with dark crinkly hair, and who stood over seven feet tall. This intruder—if that he really be—wore huge, hand-sewn boots, trousers of tent-canvas, and, oddly, an overlarge long-sleeved shirt buttoned tightly at the collar and cuffs in spite of the day's warmth.

Rufus' eyes slowly opened wide enough as to be lidless, and he choked out this fear-imbued acknowledgment: "Yuh-yuh-yuh-yuh...*yew*..."

The colossan responded, "'T'would only be a man with a soul made'a pig shit ta dew suthin' to a gull like what *ye're* doin' ta that 'un," yet the vociferation sounded unrepresentative of any human voice to ever register in Rufus' ears. The words issued resonant yet shallow; tenuous yet at the same time deep as a basso choirist; and, ever more odd, *mumbly* as though the heavily lipped mouth were attempting to speak around solid obstacles; or as if the vocal organs themselves suffered from some manner of maladaptation.

In truth, however, the voice could be better described, to those more imaginative, as otherworldly.

Rufus, even in spite of his urine-releasing fear, found

himself able to challenge, "Yew're thet warlock's grandkid, and thet retart witch Lavinny's son!"

The titan intruder stared, his face obscured by half-shadows.

"An'-an'-an'-they'se ben some *kids* missin' thet them daown at Osborn's say *yew* snatched—fer warlockin'n' *spells!*"

"Dun't talk of what ye know nuthin' abaout," responded the peculiar voice.

"An'-an'-an'...yew kilt my *dog!*"

"Yer dog all savage and askew in its head from bad raisin'—like ye. *Lotta* dogs like that raound heer—so's I kill 'em. Whether a man or a dog, if it's ugly in its head, it dun't desarve ta be a-livin'. Kilt a Hutchins' dog, wal, ten yeer ago, too, 'cos it were jess as crazy as this 'un. Made me happy, it did, to feed that animal's carcass ta the hogs. T'would make me jess as happy ta do likewise with ye. "

Rufus began to crawl backward, absorbing the monstrosity's implication. "Daon't yew do nuthin' ta me! My pa'll come awf-tuh yew!"

Some perverted facsimile of a chuckle escaped the giant's lips. "Yer pa say the same thing way back when, and he in a wheelchar naow. But dun't worry—I en't gonna kill ye"—then, with a remarkable agility, the tall shape reached down with speed like a mouse trap, snapped a hand to Rufus' bare groin—"but it weren't good to see what yew were a-doin' ta that gull, so's I figger it best ta crunch these up, on accaount the likes'a ye dun't need ta be reproducin' none"—and then, amid a grisly and most noisome sound, crushed Rufus' testicles within the scrotal sack.

Rufus' vocal reaction was less like a man's scream and more like the outright caterwaul of some beast of Mastodonic proportions. He bucked against the ground, his plentiful body-fat jiggling. The colossan felt the ruffian's testes begrudgingly divide and sub-divide into cohered chunks, then said chunks were fractionated as well, until only an oatmeal-like slush remained extant within the malodorous scrotum.

The desired effect was, hence, achieved; the giant figure's

18

actions left Rufus transformed into *pain incarnate.* He flopped ludicrously on the ground as his caterwaul sputtered down; then, with a face ballooned and reddened, he began a haphazard crawl over the fence, his trousers still down, and one hand to the ill-treated scrotum. Agony hoarsened his words: "I'se a-tellin' my pa'n my Uncle Will, tew!"

"Jess ye dew that," the titan replied in a clipped garble, "an' I'll kill 'em, an' ye're mama as well. She ought be 'shamed of herself for birthin' a boy like ye."

Rufus crawled away, sobbing.

It was then that the towering, oddly proportioned figure, who'd effectively saved Sary from sure peril, turned.

"Hi," he said.

Sary shivered, naked but no longer terrified in spite of her rescuer's physical and—in particular—facial aspect, for that aspect would be found by most to be extraordinarily terrifying: chinless, elongated as if vised, sporting a rowdy beard, skin of forehead and cheeks large-pored and yellow quite like fresh-plucked chicken skin.

Sary wasn't sure how to cogitate this situation; what she felt with the most immediacy, however, was gratitude. She dragged herself up to a sitting position, and offered, "Hi. And thank yew much fer sendin' that Hutchins boy away—"

"Never like that boy," came the sonorous voice. "All evil in his head, he is, like his whole family. Warn't good ta see him doin' such things ta ye—" The voice drifted as the giant's eyes seemed to quell an inner rage. "Folks is jess...so bad raound these parts it seems."

Sary replied cheerily, "Oh, they sure is—some'a the wust folks ever."

"Heer," and then the giant's hand, timidly as if conscious of a desire not to alarm her, lowered, a clean handkerchief in it. "Why'n't you let me wipe that ugly boy's snot off'a ye." Sary stiffened, then sighed a relieving sigh, as the gesture cleaned the mucous from her face.

"Thuh-thank yew." She sat up, unabashed at her near nudity. The titan man seemed to take downcast glances at her body. Sary knew her face was hideous but knew also that men

19

liked her body, and since this man had in all probability saved her life, it only seemed fair that she allow him to engage in coitus at no charge. She spread her legs and ran a hand through the profusion of coal-black private hair. "Can't think'a no other way ta shew my proper gratitude 'sept ta let'cha fuck me, so go on ahead, if yew've a mind tew."

Her colossal rescuer stood awkwardly in a long pause as the lowering sun beamed behind his head, eclipsing him. Sary could not compute a reason, though she felt with certainty that the man was suddenly uncomfortable. "Naw, wouldn't be right nor decent considerin' what'cha jess been through."

"Huh?"

His strange yet interesting half-garble lowered. "Wouldn't feel good in my heart doin' suthin' ta ye that ye didn't likewise have a want for. I calc'late yew're aout'a sorts by what that fat boy'n his dog was puttin' ta ye."

Sary could not conceive of such words coming from local rustics; indeed, if anything, the local men at large seemed exclusively to exhibit a flagrant if not *innate* bankruptcy of all moral ethos. Instead, she sat inclined, breasts healthily plumpened, and she stared with puzzlement at the sun-halo'd black cut-out head. She could surmise no response to his explication.

"But naow, if ye'd like, ye can come back whar I live'n have a rest, and-and, I see that black-hearted boy done tore yer gown, so's I can stitch it back for ye on accaount my mother larnt me haow ta sew."

Sary felt beside herself. Any other denizen of Dunwich, she knew, would be on top of her already, but here instead was this strange fellow offering her a place to rest and to mend her gown. *Can't believe what I'm heerin',* she thought.

The man went on in some indefinable excitement: "Oh, ee-yuh, and I'se also got a bunch'a white-tail rabbit in the smoker which I hand-rubbed fust with seasonin' like from my grandmother's recipe. It's quite fine, it 'tis, in the event that yew're hungry."

And now the endowment of a free meal! Aside from some raspberries filched from Frye's fields, and a luckily stumbled-

upon radish that had most likely fallen off a motor-truck, Sary
had consumed no solid food for over a day; and, hence—not
taking into account the ejaculations of several oral suitors—
no other sustenance. She nearly lost her breath over the giant's
charitability. "Oh, I would jess *love* that!" she wailed, hauling
her ravaged gown back down.

It was sensed more than espied a desperate smile come
to her rescuer's face. "Heer, lemme help ya up," and then the
hand at the end of the very long arm clasped her own. "Theer
yew go—"

But when Sary was left to stand upon her feet, she teetered
in place, cried "Aw, buggers!" and would've fallen over had
not the colossan caught her in a misproportioned arm.

"Yew all right?"

"My, I— I got all a-wobbly in my knees," she replied in
his embrace. "I guess what that boy were doin' left me more
shook up'n I thought—"

"'Tis understantable, but dun't worry. I'll carry ye."

Sary felt levitating as the giant cradled her up in his
arms and, as though her weight were no more a burden than
an empty potato satchel, stepped over the low stone fence
and loped toward the distant easterly tree line. Sary made a
pleasant moan in her throat; for once, she felt safe. She lolled
in the cradle of her carrier's arms, rocking gently with each
loping step.

As he conducted her across the field, her eyes scanned
her surroundings. A more beautiful day could not have been
wished for, she mused, but then when her gaze stopped upon
the sheer face of the distant Round Mountain, her appreciation
of natural beauty retarded a gobbet; closer in the distance, she
spied the several odd round hills most of whose tops were
barren of trees and displayed instead peculiar arrangements
of stone columns that she'd heard went back to Indian days.
She'd also heard that the loftiest of these hills—*Sentinel* Hill—
boasted an altar of some sort, which had existed there "Sinct
afore the time white folk come ta this land from acrost the Big
Water," her mother had said, "for a amaount'a time longer'n
ye're head can understand." But when Sary made inquiry as

to the precise *nature* of this altar, her mother had gone silent. There were several times, too, when Sary had attempted to hike all the way to the summit, to bear witness of the altar for herself, but she always fled back in the direction she'd come, for the emanation of the strangest sounds, sounds that urged her to think that words were actually being uttered *beneath the ground...*

It was in a place well behind her that she put the unsettling thoughts, to enjoy this moment of comfort. The rent in her gown betrayed a breast, and when she glanced errantly up, she captured the giant's big, dark, and somehow sensitive eyes seeming to marvel upon its shape, but then they flicked away. It was an ordinary thing for men to look approvingly at Sary's body, a gesture which she, in secret, loathed, for such glances reminded her of her father; now, however?

The notion of this unusual man's appraisal...charmed her.

From the first, a shyness, a *tongue-tiedness,* was intimated—a *gentleness,* even, in spite of the potential terror that his unnaturally overgrown physique commanded. Yet, the query whirred at the most rearward portion of her cognizance: what might the day's *remainder* bring?

"Haow silly'a me!" she chirped. "Hope ya dun't think me rude. Yew gone ta all'a that trouble helpin' me and heer I am not even tellin' ya my name! It's Sary!"

His eyes seemed to float all about her. "Ee-yuh, I know it."

"Yew dew?"

"Wal, sure. I seen ye heer'n thar."

"Whar?"

The man shrugged, now maintaining a forward gaze. "See ye strollin' past Sawyer's cow field on occasion, and Ten Acre Meadows, and comin' out the old covered bridge a number'a times when I be up in the hills, the bridge that branch off the Aylesbury Pike." He loped on, the large boots crunching down knee-high grass. "Maybe just a week past, I seen Doc Houghton droppin' ye off at Dean's Corners after givin' yew a ride in his fancy motor."

"Oh, yeah, Doc Houghton. He gimme a ride ever so often," Sary acknowledged, and to refer to his motor-car as "fancy" was no magnification of the truth; a *Duesenberg,* he'd called it. It was Sary's understanding that Dr. Houghton enjoyed some success in his trade, more so than one would expect of a simple country physician. Still, rumors circulated that the good doctor supplemented his income handsomely by, one, foreshortening the lives of the elderly at the financial behest of relatives in wait of inheritance and, two, the drastically illegal termination of pregnancies. And while she did acknowledge that the doctor had given her much-needed rides in his exorbitant motor, she did *not* acknowledge that, with some frequency—and for a princely two dollars, no less—he bid her to his home in Aylesbury for the expressed purpose of masturbating as he half-stood on his head, while Sary slid a disturbingly stout mattock handle in and out of his anus and smacked his testicles with her opened palm. The sought-after climax involved the redeposition of his semen from his penis to his mouth.

No. Sary did not acknowledge *that.*

"I've know him for a spell," was all she said in augmentation.

"So I figgered," said her carrier next, "and since I knowed him myself on account 'twas him who come to the haouse when my grandsire was a-dyin', I didn't see no harm in my askin' him what it 'tis you're called, so's he tolt me. He tolt me 'Sary.' Oh, and I seen ye onct, tew, last yeer, when I was comin' daown off'a Sentinel Hill. You were swimmin' in the lily pond 'tween the Corey's'n the ole mill ruins."

"Yeah. I warsh there when I can, when it en't tew cold..."

"But it weren't on purpose, mind ye," the man seemed to add with some haste. "I can't have ye thinkin' I were watchin' yew with any bad intentfulness. Jess happened ta see ye when I was comin' daown."

The implication made her smile, and she actually touched his hand. "That's okay. Lotta fellas seen me with nothin' on. But I can tell, yew wouldn't watch me on purpose, not all sneaky like."

The man, oddly, seemed to gulp. "Hard not tew, I'll-I'll admit ta ye, though, 'cos I can't lie to good folks. Naow, bad folks, wal, I reckon it en't no transgression ta lie ta *them...*"

Sary peered at the words. "What'cha mean by *that?*"

"Wal, bad folks, see, they lie ta me withaout thinkin', so's it's only fittin'—"

"No, no," came her interruption. "I lie tew bad folks ever chance I get. But what'cha mean by haow it's hard not tew? Hard not tew *what?*"

Several more sturdy lopes of contemplative silence. Was it the heat of the day that broke beads of perspiration out on his forehead? "Hard *not* ta look at a gull naked when she be beautiful as ye."

Sary lay numb in her hammock of strong forearms. Scarcely in her entire life had she been complimented, save for infrequent endorsements of "customers" with regard to the skillfulness and even ingeniousness she demonstrated via certain of her carnal modus. One time Elmer Frye retailed to her: "Stew Face, yew could coax a nut aout a dead man's dick, yew could"; once, also, "En't nevuh cum so fine in all'a my life as I jess did naow, gull. If yew're face warn't so Gawd-damn *awful* on the eye, why, I'd wring my flop-tit wife's fat neck'n marry *yew!*" So much for the compliments directed toward "Stew Face." This man seemed much nicer, however, which he'd made evident thus far, not to mention some subjective component about his tenue that she ascertained via her intuitions. Finally came her reply: "Oh, yeah, I know fellas find it pleasin' to look at my body withaout no clothes on. Jess not my face."

The man halted as if bidden by an inner quandary; he looked at her with directness, in her face. "En't jess ye're body I'm talkin' abaount, no. Ye're face, tew. *All* 'a ye."

Sary felt a tempest in her head. What benefit could there be in his making false statements to her? What strategy could exist through inauthentic compliments to potentially make her compliant for sex, when that she'd already offered? *This fella could'a fucked the tar aout'a me whethers I fancied it or not,* she reminded herself. What he'd just communicated comprised, indeed, the kindest words ever spoken to her. "Ee-yuh." Again, he redirected his gaze ahead. He whispered,

"Ye're jess...so...beautiful...," and then recommenced in his steady, long-strided lope across the field.

A mile must've passed behind them in which she rode in silence, antsy, confused. Sary, in fact, felt as though she understood nothing at this moment, save for one verity. Being in his arms, feeling shielded from all harm, furnished to her an emotion that scarcely visited her bleak existence: happiness.

A second mile must've lapsed when she thought to ask, "Hey! I'se forgot! What's *yew're* name?"

"Wilbur," the deep, warbling voice informed her. "Wilbur Whateley."

THREE

July 28, 1928

My fear now iz it will get too big to keep contained by time Equinox comes round. Sinse I fail at Miskatonic, I had no choice but to make the trip to Cambridge and ast to copy their version of p. 751 of the Latin. But they treat me the same, and I calculate it was Armitage who told em to do just that. May Yog-Sothoth blast that man and throw his body evurlasting into the Basin of the Shoggoths. What difference it make to Armitage? Just another fool like the others, cant understand bout someone who look and think different. But now I keep hearin my grandsire's words—what he last say to me that night just bfore the Whippoorwills try and get him, "More space, Willy!" he say a-gaspin, "more space soon! Yew grow—an' THAT grows faster." Well, I done what he told me...but that One inside just keep growing. Got to keep it qwelled, keep its size down so it dont bust quarters afore the time. Have been feeding it smaller varmints, no more of Sawyer's Alderney cows.

Getting nervous. I maye have thougt out things improper. If only Grandfather hadnt up and die.

It all be in the house now, whole house, like Grandfather want. Was easy tearing out the ceiling and planking all the windows and doors. I got the old tore out wood in a big pile in back but I know the town folk are talkin bout it. Some of them creep up at night, they do, lookin, snoopin. I live in the sheds now, so Im sure they see that. It can only be the most stalwurt of em, though, for the thing's drippings have gotten more volumous, raising more and more a its smell. Somtimes when I see these folks and their snoopin, I'll read one of the Alko Hexes that putts on em the burdin of nawwzeeating dreams, or give em blood in their pee and cum.

26

I pray ta Yog-Sothoth on High fer His wisdom. I hope He help me do it all right at the right time.

Best thing that happen today was I finally meet her, Sary. Was the fattest a the Hutchins boys trine to hurt her and fuck her aginst her will. Made her take his dog's dick inner mouth an it made me so mad. Wanted to kill that boy butt thouht it best to bust up his nuts and give him pain like he never know. Kilt the dog, shot it. Remind me when I kild the Hutchins colly Jack back in 1916. Elam Hutchins promise ta kill me fer it but a while laytur I see him rimmin one of his wells so I walk up till I'm standin over 10 cubits off and he starts a-railin at me and shakin his fist so I jest smyle and recite one of the Ambulation Spells from p. 124 of Remigius Secret Chapter, and I red it in the Eltdown Langwidge, so it work extra good, just like Grandfather say. Elam fall right into that wellhole, he did. He still alive today but lives in one of them chairs with wheels. I no he wont do nuthing bout me nooterin his boy, for feer of what I'd do ta his hole family.

But Sary. She sleepin on my cot jess behind me, wearin my Mother's black dress. I sit heer writing an keep lookin back at her laying so beautiful like that. Erlier while she be asleep I went out an bring back the dog carcass n feed it to that One inside. But before I come back in the toolhouse ta write this I got thinkin about Sary and got all hot till I cudn't stand it any mor so I had to make my seed come out with my hand. Doin that a lot sincce that first time I see her at the pond. Cant help it.

Sary's so beautiful. She all low feeling bout how her face look but I cant calclate what she meens. It's ALL uv her that's beautiful, even her voyce, even her name. She make all that's round her beautiful jest by standing theer. Way I feel about her is sumpthin I never felt before, ever.

So far nothin bad happen. Thoght she wudn't want to come back hear cuzza me but that didnt happen, then I think shee'd wanna leave right off on account of the powerful smell of that One's drippings. I mention it—the smell, nott that One insyde— but—praise the name of Him Who Is Not To Be Named—Sary tell that becuz of a ailmint when she was a tot, she got no sense a smell at all! I know that Yog-Sothoth is blessin me.

27

Leest for today, I guess. Must stay humble an keeep wurthy. What I want more then anything is ta open the Gate proper for Yog-Sothoth, but the onlee thing I want below that is for Sary ta have good feelings about me. I'd give anything for her to feel about me what I feel thinkin bout her. I could do it with one of the spells in the Von Prinn but that woudn't bee honest. She a good person in a whole range of bad folks. Would be false for me to MAKE her have a fancy for me cuzza a spell.

But when we'd got bak, I fed her, fixt her tore gown, then we talkt some which was nice. Got distrakted, though, bein' so close ta her after pinin so long. She's so nice, so wunderfull.

She's still now. I jess look at her and smile.

Got that hot sence agin tingling below. I'll hafta go out and beat off myself again. When I do it while thinkin about her, it feel so mutch better, and all I can ponder is what it ud feel like if SHE made it come out. Hard too even reckon it.

But thatll not happen. Got to be reelistik. Got past the smell part but theres still ME. I know I don't look like NUTHIN like men hereabouts under my garments. If Sary ever wan ta do it with me, what ud she think lookin at my body with no clothes on? She'd likely run out skreemin.

In the name uv the Shining Trapezohedron! Everything bout Sary, not just her bodee but all of her, when I think of it, I get this stranje, warm, confoundin feelin in the place where I gess my hart is.

Pleese, Yog-Sothoth. Hear my prayer.

FOUR

Never before had Sary laid eyes upon this particular house, which was reasonable inasmuch as the manner in which it seemed to hide furtively behind the hill. Betraying not even an inkling of fatigue, Wilbur had transported her in his arms a considerable distance until he'd turned into the wooded fringe that half-circumscribed the Whateley property. The house had quite oddly been built right into the weedy, rock-knobbed hill itself, nearly as though the hill were attempting to consume it. Ramshackle barns, most with concaved roofs, sat greyly and decrepitly farther out, while closer stood several aged but sturdy sheds, one of which released a plume of sooty smoke—Sary estimated this to be the previously remarked upon smokehouse.

"Heer it 'tis," said her tireless bearer. "Property been in the family for couple'a centuries. See, thar be lots'a Whateleys raound heer but the fust, comin' direct from Salem, built *this* haouse."

"Waow. Two centuries, yew say?"

"Ee-yuh. That'n more."

So complacent was Sary just then that she'd heretofore remained insensible of the dwelling's most irregular feature: "Why—Wilbur. Why's all the winders of yew're haouse boarded up?"

Slowing his pace, the giant deliberated amid a pause, then adduced, "Wal, see, I dun't live in the big haouse no more"— and upon this curious statement, his steps veered away from the edifice, to approach the most substantial of the sheds. "Haven't for a spell. 'Tis this tool-haouse I live in. It be plenty sizable."

But Sary eyed the house proper as she was carried past it.

"And I'se boarded up them winders and doors on

29

accaount'a I dun't want no thievin' folks a-breakin' in. Lots'a them raound heer—*reprobate scum,* my grandsire called 'em. Ever naow'n then I see one mopin' abaout. So the haouse jess be used for storage naow—"

At the moment of this verbal revelation, the looming house seemed to emit a series of hefty creaks, a *thunk!* and then—

Sary flinched in Wilbur's arms.

—a sound that could best be detailed as a phlegmatic *snuffle,* akin to that of swine, only of incredible sonic proportions, something almost elephantine.

"Wilbur, yew say ya use yer haouse for *storage?*" Sary felt predisposed to ask. "Is it animals yew're storin' in thar?"

"Uh, ee-yuh..." He kept his gaze straight ahead. "Of a kind."

Due to his extraordinary height, Wilbur had to bend over in order to enter the tool shed. Sary found the structure commodious indeed, yet strangely lacking in the implements of its namesake. Bookshelves, instead, hung where one would surely expect tool boards to be evidenced. Only the most diminutive windows emitted the light of day, while candles sat perched abundantly about. A woodstove, cold now due to the season, sat bulkily erected in one dim corner, and another corner was occupied by a vast, intricately carved writing desk full of letter slots and tiny drawers. The desk stood nearly as tall as the man who attested to live here.

Wilbur gently put Sary down on her feet. "Knees still a-wobblin'?"

"Naw, I feel much better naow—thanks! My, '*tis* a big place, as yew said," Sary remarked, reveling in a mental luxury of having an abode similarly sized and equipped to sleep in. "En't never seed a woodstove so big neither. But... what's 'hind that cartin theer?"

The wood floor creaked as Wilbur stepped toward the indicated curtain, which he withdrew. "Warshin' cove, see?"

"Waow!" exclaimed Sary, for she'd never seen an apparatus so extensive, which consisted of a wide tin tub to stand in, surrounded by an oak frame of some craft. A length of sisal rope, serving in the function of a cable, rose from a wooden lever to a watering can on an axle mounted between two studs of the frame. Another lever, lower, sprouted from a hand-pump, servicing a narrow rubber hose which conveyed water from a large barrel all the way up to the watering can.

"A *shower's* what it's called," Wilbur reported, then stooped to demonstrate. "Fust ye work this pump till the can up top sturt a-tricklin' doawn. 'Tis a real spring barrel we gots so dun't worry none 'baout usin' water—in the winter we'se jess heat the water up fust. Then when ye're ready"—his hand indicated the higher lever—"jess pull this so's the water'll come daown on ye."

"I en't never got to warsh so fancified!" Sary celebrated. "Jess ponds or warsh tubs."

"Ee-yuh. 'T'were my grandsire built it, fer me mainly, on accaount I'se got ta warsh three times daily."

"Three times!"

"Ee-yuh. See...wal, suthin' 'baout me that give me a smell stronger'n most folks. Grandfather say I'se"—the giant paused to deliberate upon a word—"he say I best be...*inconspicuous,* which mean I shouldn't be obvious ta folks hereabouts. The smell's even wuss abaout the house—I'se surprised ye didn't make no mention of it. Hope it en't botherin' ye."

"What? Smell?" replied Sary inattentively, for she remained rapt upon the elaborate washing instrument. "I *carn't* smell. Don't really even know what smell is 'cept what my ma 'splain to me. 'Tis like tastin' and hearin' and seein' only through yew're nose. But I en't got it 'cos of a 'fection when I was little."

Wilbur peered down. "Got ye no sense of smell, you say?"

"Naw, none."

Was the tall man shivering in place, his stout lower lip trembling? Near as Sary could ascertain, the paltry information regarding her lack of an olfactory sense had left Wilbur shocked in the best of ways. Eventually he recovered from his silent jubilation. Now his hand offered a grayish lump. "Oh, and heer's some soap—"

"Soap!" she squealed.

"Ee-yuh. My grandsire larn't me haow tew make it—

simple, really. Jess boil animal fat with ashes from burnt leaves, then ye cook it daown till this is left. It work fine."

Sary perceived the bizarre washing erection as an object of enthrallment, and the soap a delicacy.

"Hot day like this I figger ye might have a hanker for a shower." Wilbur's unusual eyes seemed to sense the young woman's intrigue. His large, long-fingered hand pulled back the curtain. "Go on, step on in, then I'll close the cartin for yer privacery, and ye can get yourself aout'a that dress so's I can sew it fer ye."

Sary's molested face turned up with a smile of excitement; she stepped right in the tub, holding the piece of soap as if it were an exotic bauble. It had slipped her mind to close the curtain as per Wilbur's suggestion; instead she pulled the torn gown up over her head and off, then turned obliviously naked and handed it to him.

The giant man seemed to flinch—did he even close his eyes? She placed the gown in his hand. *He bashful 'baout seein' a gal with no clothes on?* came the curiosity. Nevertheless, she closed the curtain. Most men reveled to espy her nude; again, here was an example of his previous gentlemanliness of which most male Dunwichers had not a trace. "'Preciate ya lettin' me do this," she said behind the crude curtain. "And mendin' my gaown."

"'Tis a pleasure..."

Sary eyed the shower's pump and lever, trying to renovate in her mind the odd, tall man's operating instructions. *The pump,* she recalled. Her breasts dipped as she bent to go through the proper motions, listening to the modest gush as the sprinkling can filled over her head. Yes, it would be nice to be clean, a condition she rarely got to enjoy. Next, she eyed the lever. *What he say? Pull that, then the water come daown on me?* But as she reached to do so, she at once became aware of...

Trailing down her bare shoulders and upper chest she couldn't help but notice the countless minuscule black dots, like someone had sprinkled flecks of pepper on her. Only...

The black "flecks" were moving.

Indeed, as if in a mass exodus, these flecks (which only now did she realize were the legion of fleas and lice that took up constant residence in her scalp) were making a prompt departure from their abode. Lice and various other body vermin brought her no shame simply due to the universal fact that nearly everyone had them, and so Sary had for as long as her mind enabled her to recall. The itching one grew used to quite quickly. Yet, now, with an analogous quickness, the vermin were retreating from her. A similar exodus, then, was noticed trailing down her thighs: the multitudinous pubic mites she'd grown so equally accustomed to. It proved the strangest observation, while at the same time one she was quite pleased with.

"Havin' yew'reself a muddle in thar?" resonated Wilbur's voice. "Forget haow ta work the shower?"

"Aw, no, no, Wilbur. I 'member naow," and then she eased the lever back and shot to tiptoes as the joyously refreshing torrent sprinkled down on her head and ran down her body.

Her fascination with the soap grew childlike when she glided the fragrant gray lump about, first, skin, then her hair. The smear turned to lovely suds the more she agitated them with her hands. When she was scratching the suds into her recently deloused scalp, Wilbur's heavy and oddly vibrating voice resounded yet again from behind, "I done ment yer gaown, so's naow I'll warsh it fer ye. I got suthin' for ya to whar whiles it's dryin'. I hope ye like it."

"Oh, I'm sure I will, Wilbur. Thanks!"

When nearly the entirety of her body became a suit of suds, Sary caught her hands returning to her breasts to suds them further, then her furred sex as well. A dense tingling rarely felt in her caused her already pump nipples to plump up more, and she felt a strange warmth fill her breasts themselves. More and more, then, she caught her fingers delving as deep as their length would permit into the soft channel of her vagina. The sensations intoxicated her. Inconscient of any forethought, then, she meekly called out, "Wilbur?"

"Ee-yuh?"

"Only place on me I carn't warsh is my back. Could yew do it for me?"

A long pause ensued, then Wilbur's large frame was heard rising, his unduly sizable feet thumping toward the curtain. "Sure, if ye like. I'll just put my hand in so's ye dun't have to open the—" but Sary had already drawn the curtain open, standing naked and suds-encloaked with her back to him. Wilbur released something akin to a pleased sigh. Her small hand reached rearward until his much larger hand took the lump of ash soap. Another pause ensued: she guessed either reluctance or more likely another example of his bashfulness, then she suddenly sucked in a breath between her tongue touching the roof of her mouth when she felt her uncharacteristic rescuer begin to glide the soap up and down over her back.

"That feels soooo nice," she uttered.

He withheld any response, just kept gliding the ash soap up and down.

Then, unable to control herself, "Lower please, if ya dun't mind."

"Yuh-yuh-yuh...ya mean ye're backside too?"

Sary nodded. Of course, she'd already cleansed this region, but the feel of his strong and unusually long fingers beguiled her to make the redundant request. She leaned forward now, bracing the wood beam which supported the sprinkling can. She parted her legs.

Two long fingers of Wilbur's hand now ran up and down through the groove of Sary's buttocks; and in response, her buttocks repeatedly clenched and released. So long those fingers were—the middle one seven inches long at least, she'd previously noticed, and their companions not much shorter—and this fact only forced a consideration of fantasy: how potent a joy it would be for her to feel one of those fingers slip unhesitantly into her anus, while another slipped up into her sex. Thinking of this, in fact, caused her vaginal muscles to pulse in pre-orgasm. The fantasy turned so dense now that Sary felt not quite in her proper awareness, and she was even about to ask him to do this, but—

His huge, sudsy hand withdrew. "Thar. All nice'n clean naow?"

Sary could've toppled over. Heart drumming, and the nerves of her breasts and sex asquirm, she replied. "Thuh... thank yew, yes..."

Her lust-gauzed vision glimpsed Wilbur's hand hanging a plush white towel on a peg. "Ye rinse off naow and dry yourself," and then he closed the curtain behind her.

An actual orgasm was an experience so far removed from her that she couldn't even contemplate the last time she'd had one. The rampant sexual abuse from her father as well as the suitors of her trade delivered no such delights. *But...Wilbur...,* she mused. His unnaturally large hands on her, and those impossible fingers running between her legs... The sensation left her desperate as a weasel cornered with a pitchfork, to bring her own hands to her sex right this moment and make herself climax.

The gums of her missing front teeth clasped down on her lip; her sex continued to beat. Sary knew that if she masturbated even behind the curtain, she'd generate enough noise to alarm Wilbur.

She slumped in a tingling frustration, pulled the can-lever, and rinsed all the suds off.

After drying herself, she wrapped the towel about her body and stepped out of the metal tub. Wilbur now stood nearly stooped over, hanging up Sary's stitched-back-to-rights gown up on a window peg.

"Wow," she said, "yew fixed'n warshed my dress that fast?"

"Warn't no trouble. Hope ye liked your shower."

"I sure did!" she couldn't have replied with more enthusiasm. "I en't felt this squeaky clean since I was real little, when my ma'd scrub me in the tub." The remembrance of her mother brought a great smile to her mauled face, but in a moment more, the smile corroded.

"But now that I think back, lot'a them times my ma were warshing me? My father'd come in then, and..." She felt like some flimsy building about to collapse. "Aw, never mind."

"Wun't a good man, I take it?"

Sary shook her head quickly then sat down on a handmade

footstool and began to rub her hair dry. She didn't notice; however, after her brief reference to her father, the look in Wilbur's eyes turned to an aspect of perfect disdain. The sour moment bothered her; she struggled to change topics. "Aw, yew know what? 'T'were the funniest thing. Once I step in the shower all my body bugs run off me and go daown the drain, even afore I started warshin myself. Top'a my head dun't itch no more."

Wilbur rummaged in a storage crate set on end, which sufficed for a closet. "Ee-yuh. The bugs most folks got dun't afflict us heer. Likely, ye noticed theer en't no trace of maouse droppin's or rat holes, neither, and ye'll never see no spiders and such araound." He seemed to hunt with deliberation for something in the make-shift closet. "No critters outside, neither, not fer hunnerts of ells; 'tis why I gotta set my traps ways on aout in the woods."

"No critters outside?" she asked with emphasis.

Wilbur's big crinkly-haired head shook to indicate the negative. "No bugs, no critters, no worms—nuthin'. Nuthin' like that come on the property, and 'tis been that way sinct me and—" but here Wilbur's speculation held in momentary check, as if he were considering a more desirable choice of words. "Not sinct I were born, my grandsire say. He say it jess might be on acaount of, wal, haow I got me a more powerful smell than folks hereabaouts."

"What abaout that big haouse'a yours that yew use for storage naow? Any varmints in thar?"

"No," Wilbur said in a dry croak as though some inner monitor signaled a sign of dissembled distress. But then he turned, seeming not distressed in the least, and held out on a hanger a long diaphanous black gown that shined unlike any fabric Sary had ever beheld.

A breath lodged in her chest. "That en't fer me ta whar, is it?"

"It sure enough is. 'Twas my mother's... Yew'd do it service ta wear it."

Sary was awestruck; never in her life had she seen much less worn such a beautiful garment.

"And it en't yours jess to wear, mind ya. It's fer ye to have."

Calculating his words took time. This she could not believe. "Wilbur, I could never take this fine dress as a gift."

"'Tis yours naow." He smiled crookedly but veritably, then placed the shimmering gown across her arms. "Why dun't ye put it on while's I go fetch our supper aout the smoker?" and with that, he thunked out of the shed and closed the door.

A corner of Sary's eye effused a single tear. No doubt existed. This was the nicest day she'd ever been blessed enough to live.

FIVE

At the finish of a meal she might refer to as sumptuous (had the word existed in her vocabulary), Wilbur had tended to her remaining ear with some manner of poultice saturated with a mucilaginous medicine that he'd owned, "'Tis'll take the pain right off, and heal them bitemarks up. My grandsire tell me he get this from *his* grandsire, so's ye can bet it's old. Old-time medicine's better'n new."

The pain, indeed, dissipated immediately. "It's workin', all right—thanks!" Sary said.

Wilbur applied some tape to hold the poultice in place, and promised, "Ye'll be fine in a jiffy. If ye're wonderin', this be nothin' scarcely more than some mashed up tar root."

"That's all?" Sary questioned.

"Wal, plus mixed in is a bit'a this and a dab'a that," and he pointed to a glass cabinet full of small old-style medicine bottles. "Locust juice, snake heart, blue iris petals. It wucks, it does. Jess ye wait."

Sary wasn't sure but she thought she glimpsed a few bottles of preserved toads, salamanders, and bats as well.

With Wilbur's first aid complete, the two of them engaged in further discourse, then, more full-bellied than she'd been in distant memory, Sary yawned. The day still shined brightly beyond the small, high windows, yet Wilbur needed no further clue to sense that she was whelmed by fatigue. He pointed to a mattressed cot beside the high desk. This was obviously where Wilbur slept, for the crude but precisely constructed low table at the cot's end demonstrated the extra length needed for his abnormally long legs. "You're bushed, Sary, I'se kin tell, so jess ye go on'n have yerself a nap while I run some errands."

The idea of a nap, after the luxuriant shower and then huge helpings of exquisitely seasoned smoked meats, sounded

38

lovely to her, but— "Aw, no, that'd be rude after all yew done fer me. I'll help ya with your errands."

Wilbur's head shook in a manner that was not dominating at all but insistent just the same. "Git ye some rest. I wun't lollygag so's ta leave ye alone too long."

Sary yawned again, bringing one fist to her puff-lipped mouth, then stretching her arms in the extravagant black dress. "Wal, okay. Thanks. I am tired all's a suddent."

Pleased, Wilbur took his leave of the shed. Even behind the heavy wood door, his enormous booted feet could be heard thudding the ground. But just as Sary would venture to the long, appended cot, her fatigue was instantly superimposed by an irresistible inquisitiveness. Her feet took her timidly about the structure's cramped interior. She glimpsed some sheets of handwriting in a binder on the desk, and though Sary did have some reading skills, thanks to her mother's diligence, she could make nothing of the unintelligible scribblings. They were more than simply words she'd never seen, but instead unlike words at all.

Rows of hoary books filled a handmade shelf, and atop a table of heavy oak, amid some scatterings of papers, sat a thick, iron-hinged tome that looked ancient. If there'd been a title on the cover, age and considerable wear had removed all vestige. Although Sary knew she shouldn't—the book was not hers, nor any of her business—she gently lifted the stout cover, hearing its hinges grind, and, with some difficulty, read this:

NECRONOMICON
Ye Booke of Laws of ye Dead

As record'd by Abdul Al-Hazred,
Mad Arab of Damascus
Translat'd from the Latin of Olaus Wormius
by Dr. John Dee
for Her Majesty the Queen,
Elizabeth the First

London, 1582

39

Edward Lee

Strips of thin leather marked certain places in the age-plumpened book: she turned to one, and found herself on page 751. So ancient was the paper that it reminded her of the softness of felt, yet worm-holes pocked the sheet like overlarge flyspecks. Sary could only read one line before a nauseousness rushed to her stomach:

...be thee One of Fayth, thou shalt hear Their Gibbers from deepe beneath ye Ground and amid ye Stonie Places of Reverence where ye sanctified words hath been spake, and, yea, high up from ye Heavens; if thee be estimat'd to be Worthie of Their observance. Hark! Yog-sothoth be ye key, and unto ye faythfull, forsooth, yog-sothoth wilt smile...

Stalwart Venturer, keepe thy fayth, for upon this page be ye secret—yea!—the Dho and the Dho-Hna...

Something arcane about the sentences and their fancy winged letters left a sense in Sary's brain that existed with a similitude to the taste left in her mouth several years ago when a man passing through town (Harley Warren, he'd called himself, and said he was from the South) had paid her half a dollar to suck on his anus while he partook in masturbation.

Yuck...

She closed the wretched book at once and turned away.

The recollection bothered her most, the page's references to noises "deepe beneath ye ground" and "stonie places."

Next, her eyes scanned the high, elaborate desk, a desk larger than any she'd been aware of. There was a newspaper—the *Aylesbury Transcript*—some manner of fiction magazine—*Home Brew,* dated February, 1922—a trade journal from January, 1928, called *The Nathaniel Derby Pickman Foundation,* announcing an upcoming expedition to Antarctica, a place Sary had never heard of; plus less distinct curiosa in the form of pamphlets, strips of handwritten notes, and cancelled stamps including a twenty-four-cent stamp

40

depicting an upside-down aeroplane. While Sary had heard of these inconceivable flying machines, she'd never seen one. Were they designed to fly upside-down? But more of those odd papers of indecipherable writing lay about the sliding top in a more orderly fashion. When she innocently opened one of its miniature drawers, she squinted at a small jar unto whose lid was affixed a string; from the string pendulated a lump of some dark metal, while the jar was labeled in handwriting *A. Bierce.* Behind it a second jar was found, labeled *t.o.m.* She opened another drawer but re-closed it right away with a gasp, for it contained what appeared to be the eyes and nose-cavity of a yellowed skull. No, she'd not be opening any more drawers! Yet the desk and all its Gordian complexity held her spellbound where she stood. All those letter-slots, and letters in almost all of them! Were they letters Wilbur was writing? If so, the prospect seemed irregular, for Wilbur didn't strike her as a man with many correspondents. More likely than not, they were old family letters. Her curiosity felt as one of perfect innocence when her fingers slipped a few envelopes out...

Wal, I'll be...

Sary had been wrong: the giant man who'd saved her today did indeed have others to correspond with, for the letters were all addressed to *Wilbur Whateley* of *Dunwich Village,* some dating back as far as 1920. Sary knew her curiosity would have extended too far had she removed the missives from their sheaths and read of their contents, but what harm could there be in taking notice of their return addresses?

Her eyes narrowed immediately. Two were from Miskatonic University in Arkham, a town Sary had heard of and knew to be not far distant. Another from a man in Kingston, New York, named Alonzo Typer; another from a Robert Blake in someplace called Wisconsin; and yet another from someone here in Dunwich, named Septimus Bishop, though she'd never heard of this latter man, what with so many Bishops here and there. An eyebrow popped up when she read the next return address: Innsmouth, from someone named Marsh. Sary recognized the town, for it was the only town she'd ever traveled to outside of Dunwich; her mother had taken her there once to visit a friend whom she—her mother—had grown up with. The next return address owned to no location at all but only revealed: The Church of Starry Wisdom.

So it seemed that fuddlement and nothing more would be her curiosity's prize. *I best mind my own business,* she suggested to herself. *Think I'll have a walk aoutside,* but before she got to the door, she took notice of a block-print map that read THE CAMPUS OF MISKATONIC UNIVERSITY, and crudely circled on it with pen-ink was a square which read LIBRARY. More pen-writing instructed, WATCH FER DOG and 4th WINDOW, EAST SIDE IZ CLOSEST TO RARE BOOK ROOM. Sary couldn't imagine what these notes might mean. On a small, cherrywood end-table lay another map, but this was one folded. All she could read of its front print was HARVARD UNIVERSITY, CAMBRIDGE, MASS., EST. 1636, and more scribble, WIDENER and 2nd FLOOR SPECIAL BOOKES & MSS. ROOM. More fuddled than ever, Sary turned, opened the door, and left the tool-house.

Her bare feet glided her across plush green grass; the sun beamed down, and she nearly gasped in delight when she saw how the sun's rays caught the countless glittering flecks that seemed imbued by magic into her black gown's intricate fabric. She fairly beamed herself.

A trace glance showed her several other sheds in the distance, some in bad repair, then she looked again to the well-built, tin-topped smoker-house which had provided her the delectable meal. Instinct warned her to keep mindful of those awful red ants that stung her feet to no end when she walked in the wrong places, but then relief came when she remembered Wilbur telling her that no varmints or insects existed anywhere near the Whateley property. She knew this to be true now more than ever, for not a single mosquito had bitten her yet, even though this time of season they were rife. The shadow of the vast Round Mountain interestingly cast a great darkened curve upon the forest belt beyond. The woods looked so lovely in that half-dark, half-bright line of contrast, but she declined activating her idea to take a stroll amongst the trees, for something seemed...unnatural about them. Surely she'd never observed trees so twisted, stout, and gnarled. Indeed, they appeared over-nourished, glutted, as though they'd grown for their centuries of existence via the sustenance of sour minerals in the soil. Some of the trees reminded her of monstrous figures as of those in nightmares.

Now her gaze surveyed her point of vantage in a wider arch. Beyond the side of the strangely boarded-up Whateley house, she could see the dirt road that eventually took one away from Dunwich, to the Aylesbury pike. It occurred to her to amble to the road, to see if Wilbur might be on his way back—she could greet him—but next, however, it was the dilapidated house that snagged her notice. Did some ugly, dark substance leak from its boarded windows and doors? *Like tar,* she associated. It may have been her imagination, then, when she thought she detected a single *quake* of the house itself, as if something huge within—the main timbers, perhaps—had hitched and settled. Then her memory brought back to her that brief but hideous noise she'd thought she heard earlier, a noise like a monumental *snort...*

The great abode, like the book in the shed, caused an unpleasant throb in her belly and a minute headache, so she quickly turned to be out of sight of it. But no sooner had she traversed when she noticed another oddity...

Beneath a long rickety canopy of wood-slats, cords of firewood sat neatly stacked, surely an amount that would take months of a cruel winter to deplete. But the oddity was what sat heaped in a ten-foot-high pile *next* to the firewood.

Building scrap in the manner of a great tumble of house lumber: rafters, beams, doors and their frames, wall-slats, and even great chunks of whole walls. By the looks of the pile, these materials came clearly from *interior* construction, but they'd now become subject just as clearly to an act of *de*construction, as if aspects of the interior had been sundered. *I wonder if Wilbur done knocked out all'a the walls of the big haouse...* Whatever it was he stored inside must be quite large. Why a pile of wood-scrap would instill in her a sense of foreboding she didn't know.

Pursing her lips as if at a rank sapor, she continued her meandering examination of the property.

A number of prodigious drakeberry bushes, in long ranks, diced up the grassy region just beyond the tool-house. Amid the bush by which she walked the closest, she noticed a natural indentation, like a cove of sorts, deep and tall enough for one to enter without being seen by anyone not in close proximity, and it was into this "cove" that Sary's curiosity took her next.

The cove curled inward in nearly a hook-shape, and at its furthest limit she noticed...

What's them THINGS?

A pile of singularly curious...*things* lay on the ground; Sary's immediate tendency was to divine the impression of pony stools, for they existed as roundish wads approximately an inch wide apiece. Size and shape, however, was where this similarity ended: pony stools, or any excrement that Sary knew of, always bore a rather universal brownish color, while the pile of things she looked at now were far more akin to the color of a peeled banana slightly overripe. This mystery-laden pile stood perhaps two feet in height, tapering as it ascended. Most would find the nature of the wad-like objects as unpleasant or even foul, yet Sary found them only objectively interesting, considering how accustomed her life had made her to the unpleasant, the foul, the disgusting, etc. And it was this curiosity which urged her to stoop and pick up between her fingers the topmost object...

A strange slimy texture registered immediately. When she lifted the thing she expected it to separate from the heap individually but this was not the case; instead, more of the off-white balls came with the first, and now she perceived that they were in some manner connected, as of a grotesque string of pearls. Fascination finnicked with her. She kept lifting the first ball but found that the entire queue of the others stopped at exactly ten balls. This led her to assume that the remainder of the pile existed similarly: a string of ten slimy balls deposited and redeposited over a period of time, comprising the entire heap...

Whatever could the things be?

44

Fascinated though she was, Sary ended her examination and presumed to continue visually surveying more of Wilbur's property, in which, after taking leave of the bush's hidden cove, she crossed it to look around.

The latrine ditch was what she glimpsed next, along with its tightly lashed frame of logs where one would sit to defecate. It reminded her that she herself needed to urinate, but she'd always been fearful of such waste-ditches, for once her father had thrown her into one after a particularly vehement session of forced intercourse. She'd been very young at the time—six or seven—and as she recalled, his reaction had not been positive when she'd refused to lap up the traces of his semen which had leaked out of her after his climax. So it was a trip to the bottom of the latrine that was her compensation for such non-compliance.

She picked another ample drakeberry bush behind which to secret herself, then raised with care her luxurious black dress, and immediately lowered herself to a squat. It was then that all of the pleasant sensations her skin had been receptive to today...had commingled, and then intensated to an effect many times more robust: the comfort of being carried in Wilbur's strong arms, then the feel of her own hands caressing the suds of the ash soap all over her body in the shower machine, then—much more so—the feel of *Wilbur's* hands sliding up and down in the cleave of her buttocks and how she cringed for the fantasy of the elongated fingers sliding into her private orifi... Even the captivating black gown itself beguiled her in some concupiscent manner, some mystery of its fabric that felt, whenever she walked, as of the hands or even the tongue of some semi-palpable wraith tenderly stroking her skin. Foggy-eyed with these muses, a few moments passed, then her bladder began to void; the stream glittered as it arced out of her and up, and then she discovered her index and middle fingers were V'd at the folds her of sex, opening it; it was such that even the mundane function of urinating pushed more lustful desires into her head. The stream declined, then ceased, yet she remained in her lewd squat, at once finding one hand slipped into the gown's top, fondling a breast; her

45

fingers catered to the already nerve-plump nipple which sent the most delectable sensations gusting to her privates. Then she imagined Wilbur's fingers there, then his mouth, *sucking.*

Aw, durn, that feels good...

She licked the fingerpad of her other hand, stroked the pink nub of her clitoris, once very slowly, then again twice. Her body's reaction to this meager tending was an intoxicating tension; her head rolled around. Two more quicker strokes brought a pulsing outburst to her loins whose density of pleasure caused her to fall over and cringe. She twitched there on the ground, her face overcome by a smile of delight the likes of which she'd not experienced in years. The initial impulse to masturbate had been puissant enough; however, it was the fantasy of *Wilbur's* participation that had set her sexual responses off like a black-powder keg.

Sary lay sidled over awhile longer, pilfering out the last of the after-sensations, but then—

Terror came.

The unmistakable scuff of footfalls could be heard not far off. *Aw, Gawd, please let it be that no one seen me!* She jumped up (hoping that the bush's partial coverage had concealed her from the interloper) and righted her gown as best she could. Either the walker was Wilbur or it was—

Wilbur said he boarded up his haouse 'cos folks sometimes try ta break in...

Sary prayed to God that it wasn't some foul-minded Dunwich thief trespassing upon the property. If such a man saw Sary, out here all by herself?

She knew she'd be raped most dementedly.

She peeked around the edge of the bush, yet her eyes only had time to glimpse a figure turn round the hill and disappear behind the sheds, which could only mean...

He be headin' for the big house...

A daring not typically known to her had her quickly dart from the bush, past the latrine, and to the wall of the smoking-house. It was a deep breath she drew into her lungs, then... She peeked around the smoker's corner.

Thank yew, Gawd...

Relief assailed her when she easily identified the "interloper" as Wilbur himself. She was about to call out a greeting but impulse at the last moment caused her to forbear the gesture. Impulse, but also...observation.

What's that over his back?

Indeed, a sack of some kind seemed to be slung across the gargantuan man's back as he walked with deliberance toward the boarded-up house. However, Sary now discerned that one of the house's doors stood absent of the nailed planks and beams that sealed all the others and windows. Instead, it was barred by upper and lower iron struts fixed across the egress by two large and ponderous old locks. Wilbur, still not at all cognizant of Sary's vigilance, extracted a key, unfastened the locks, and opened the door...

The young woman's angle of observation afforded her a fair view into the domicile's east end, and the sunlight, though partially truncated, showed her only vast emptiness inside. *Whatever it 'tis Wilbur keep stored in thar, it gotta all be at the other end,* she deduced.

She naturally expected Wilbur to enter the leaning abode, but this he did not do. Instead, and most curiously, he remained where he stood outside, and then it looked as though he were *talking...*

Who the hail he talkin' tew if thar en't no one livin' inside? The extended distance prevented Sary's deciphering any of what her rescuer was saying.

And next?

Wilbur made the oddest gesture with his hand: at first Sary believed him to be crossing himself the way a priest or minister would, but the motions that were made indicated something far more complicated. It was only a moment later, then, that the colossan unslung the burden across his back and flung it into the house. Then he re-barred and locked the entry.

Sary's plentiful curiosity took on a tinge of something not unlike dread, for in the few seconds before Wilbur had resecured the door, she'd verified that it was no sack at all that he'd tossed within. It was a dead dog.

A dead *collie,* to be more unequivocal.

Same exact dog that awful Hutchins boy sicked on me, she knew, and how could any doubt exist? She'd seen Wilbur blow the barbarous animal's brains out with a pistol.

More strangeness, in a manner by which she could make no deductions.

She expected Wilbur to return to the tool-shed, but instead he loped straight away from the big house and into the twisted woods. *Whar's he goin' naow?* Sary meandered about the property, looking errantly at the splotches of grass and wild beds of flowers, noting again nary a sign of insect activity, and no bees rummaging for pollen. "Wal, hey thar!" Wilbur greeted her when he'd reappeared some twenty minutes later. "Hi, Wilbur. I was gettin' ta miss yew," she said, acknowledging now that his departure, admixed with the inexplicable observations she'd made, had left her vaguely unnerved. But Wilbur's big, angular face seemed to betray a hint of happiness when she'd said she missed him. "Sorry, I took a tad longer'n I thought. Ran into that bald fella, Kyler be his name—he abaout the only Dunwicher who'll share a good word with me. A *soothsayer* is what he claim he is."

The word perplexed Sary. "A sooth—*what?*"

"One who tell fortunes, like I heerd they got at curnivals. Dun't know haow true it 'tis, though."

All she could think to say was, "Carn't say I'se heerd of him, but I'm glad you got a friend." Her expression cheered. "Wal, naow ya got two friends, me bein' the second."

Wilbur's approach slowed, as more inner happiness seemed to dawn within him.

"We'll be friends, always, Sary," he replied in a solemn tone.

Wilbur was so tall that Sary unconsciously stood on tiptoes to see what he had now on his shoulder. *Not another dead dog,* she hoped, but in a moment identified a trap rope.

"So that's what yew were doin' in the woods," she observed. "Checkin' yer traps."

"Ee-yuh." He'd reached her by now and unshouldered the cord, attached to which were several squirrels, a muskrat, and a woodchuck. "A more than midland ketch today," his dark, warble of a voice reported. "En't ketched a woodchuck in spell. But like I told ye, I gotta walk aout in the wood a good distance 'cos critters dun't come near the haouse."

Sary naively wondered if he intended to deposit these animals into the big house as he'd done with the dog, but, *'A'course not. They'se for him ta put in the smoke-house,* she realized.

"Hope ye have a likin' for woodchuck."

"Oh, I dew—"

"I got a old family recipe that make it taste like duck..." A pause, then his large dark eyes blinked on an afterthought. "Aw, but ye sure didn't have yerself much of a nap, huh?"

Sary shook her head, admitting to the distraction of how glad she was to see him. "'Tis funny. Tired as I was, the minute yew left, I couldn't sleep a wink so's I just kind'a walked abaout, lookin' raound yer land. Hope ya dun't mind."

"Not one bit," Wilbur said, but he seemed distracted as well, distracted by her simple presence. His eyes persisted on her: each time he was about to speak, he stalled. "I...uh. Aw, durn, Sary..."

"What?"

"I'se jess real happy yew stayed. Whole time I was aout, I thought sure ye'd be gone time I got back..."

She grinned at the absurd remark. "Wilbur, I wouldn't just up'n leave withaout sayin' goodbye."

The huge man shuffled awkwardly in his big boots. "I know the way I look put gals off—"

"The way yew look's just fine ta me, so's I carn't think'a what yew mean," she tried to allay his faltering esteem. Yes, Wilbur's physical aspect diverged a great deal from that of other men, but Sary only found this trait unique and interesting, not repugnant. She thought, *The way my face look, no ear, all scarred 'n pocked, nose mashed up by my pa? It be a blessin' from Gawd Wilbur even turn a glance at me.* Through the self-analysis, however, she realized that not only was she comfortable with Wilbur's appearance, she felt progressively more attracted to him, this latter fact being betrayed then and there as she felt her nipples tingle and begin to stand up beneath the sheer cover of the dress.

I wonder if he notice that... However, these ruminations, though they expended only moments, left an uncomfortable silence, so she carried on her perky reply, "Yew been nicer ta me than...wal, anyone I can ever 'member meetin', and I'd never be rude so ta jess leave withaout me sayin' so fust. Naow, let me help ya git them critters skinned and gutted. No reason yew should do all this work withaout me liftin' a finger ta help."

Wilbur's colossal physique went from tense to lax. "Nup. 'Tis my job, and I'll have in done in a jiff. Why not ye jess wait fer me in the tool-haouse, take a rest?"

"Okay."

Upon the instant of returning to the shed—and with no conscious mandate whatever—Sary's hands slipped up the inside of her gown to further caress her sex. Even this long after her eruptive orgasm, the exotic pleasure lingered; she even felt as though she could masturbate again. *Jess sumpin' 'baout Wilbur got me hotter'n the top of a Dutch oven...*, but only then did she catch herself, and expeditiously withdrew her hands. What might Wilbur conclude were he to walk in suddenly?

Several minutes later, he indeed returned, ducking below the door's transom.

"That's shore a fast skinnin' and guttin' job," Sary observed. Just looking at him, however, had her painstakingly sidetracked. Why this misproportioned giant kindled her so lickerishly, she could not appraise, but she recognized this: *If thar ever be a man I'd want to lay me right daown and fuck me, why...it'd be him.*

"Been dressin' critters so long, I kin dew it in my sleep," Wilbur's voice wavered in its bizarre depth. "Say"—he stepped forward—"I bet'cher ear don't hurt naow, huh?"

The question sparked in Sary's head, as she realized his assertion was true. "Yew was right, Wilbur. I don't got no pain a'tall no more."

His huge hands rested on her shoulders, urging her toward the cot. At first, Sary's loins made a steamy, spontaneous clench; her crudest impulses hoped he meant to immediately prostrate her on the cot and *have* her, just as per her fantasy—

"Set ye daown right here," he said instead, gesturing the cot. "Gonna check it."

When seated, Sary was surprised by the daintiness with which Wilbur's enormous hands removed the poultice he'd previously applied. "Thar," he remarked in a manner that seemed proud. "All healed up, jess like I say."

Sary felt her remaining ear and easily discerned that even the dog's bite marks were healed. "That's *amazin'.* I carn't thank yew enough, Wilbur."

"Warn't nuthin'," he said, then loped toward the desk. But something caught his eye on the big table.

"Oh, I see ye took a look at the *Necronomicon.*"

"Huh?"

"The big book with the hinges," he clarified, regarding the creepy tome she'd peeked at.

"Wal, yeah," she confessed. "Hope ya en't mad—"

"Naw." He flipped to a few age-fattened pages. "Probably nuthin' in it ye'd understand no ways, nor be interested in."

Sary was relieved that he didn't consider her "peek" a trespass into his privacy. "My mother teached me ta read a little, but I couldn't make hardly nothin' aout'a all them fancy words. I just thought it was a Bible."

"Wal, it 'tis in a manner." Wilbur's peculiarly dark eyes remained focused on the pages he scanned. "Been somethin' I study quite a bit. Only problem is there be some flawed incantations."

Sary cast a querying glance. "What's that mean?"

Hinges creaked when he closed the prodigious book. "My grandsire tolt me that when this heer copy be translated inta English, someone monkeyed with the words—on purpose probably—so's ta take away the book's...what was that word he used? *Efficacy,* I think. Ee-yuh. The monkeyin' took off the book's efficacy, which means some'a its best parts wun't work."

By now, Sary's not-terribly-formidable intellect had lost all comprehension as to what the giant man might mean; but, so not to feel stupid, she merely gave a nod, and said, "Oh."

Next, Wilbur's large-pored face glanced frustratedly to the map pinned to the wall.

That college in Arkham, Sary recalled. *And sumpthin' wrote on it abaout books...*

"So's naow I got ta go back to Miskatonic and get me another look at the unflawed copy they got thar."

"Go back? Yew mean ya already been?"

"Ee-yuh. Onct." In his tone, there came a negative inference regarding the excursion. "But the man runs the library thar, he en't much. Armitage be his name. Treated me like I be scum'n sent me aout."

Sary felt badly for her friend's frustration, but all she could offer was, "Wal, then, ain't it likely he'll send ya aout again?"

Wilbur's look to her might have been called desperate and pleading. But of her question, he added nothing.

Her generally unfired libido still raged betwixt her thighs, yet other questions battled with it, questions she burned to ask. Like: what was Wilbur keeping in the big house, and why had he deposited the dead dog in it? What could account for the extensiveness of the interior planks, timbers, wall- and door-frames, etc. that had been piled outside? And—

What be them weird white ball-things in the crook of the bush?

Better judgment prevailed, however, not typical of her. *Why ask stuff that don't be none'a my business?* And in a moment, she felt her eyelids droop; a drowse was coming on with promptitude.

Wilbur had taken a seat at the big desk with all the slots. "I'll jess be a little while heer," and then he appeared— pen in hand—to devote his attention to the sheets of paper Sary had seen, those filled with writing whose words were constituted in an alphabet she'd never seen. But this was all she remembered observing before her fatigue pulled her down on the cot...

In the sweet, scintillant darkness behind her sleeping mind's eye, she dreamed of Wilbur lying beside her, kissing her...

Some time later, when her eyes fluttered open, she could tell by the tiny windows that the sun had moved considerably. She yawned and sat back up, surprised. "Why, I must'a been asleep."

"Ee-yuh," Wilbur replied. He remained scribbling at the monumental desk. "Ye needed it. 'Baout an hour ye was out, I'd say."

She felt energized now, in her mind, but also in her nerves. That dream, short and incomplete as it had been, left her nipples more gorged with excited blood than ever; it seemed impossible for Wilbur not to notice their swelling against the material of the fine, black dress. She returned her gaze to the arch-backed, intent figure at the desk...

Ever the more now, this man, Wilbur Whateley, was striking her as one of uttermost fascination.

"Must be quite a letter writer," she said from her place on the cot. "All them neat little slots is mostly full."

He replied without addressing her. "Been sendin' and gettin' lots of letters over the yeers. But this heer's just my keepin' a journal fer myself. If ye'd took a glance at it, you'd see it be writ in a secret way. A *cipher* 'tis called. My grandsire teached me, so's I could read what he left. Guess that's what I'm doin' too, leavin' a record'a such stuff as pertains to family business, suthin' that not jess anyone could read."

This Sary hardly understood, either. But her eyes held fast on the high desk. "Ain't never seen a desk so big'n interestin'."

Wilbur nodded, his fountain pen scribbling. "'Tis nice, all right. I used ta use that old bureau over thar for my desk, but then one time I were in Osborn's general store tew buy me a valise to hold papers"—without removing his eyes from the sheet, his long, stout finger indicated said valise in the corner—"ta take with me to Miskatonic that fust time I went. But out front, I spied Zech Whateley's wagon a-settin' thar with this desk in it'n a For Sale sign. So's I bought it off him. Naow, he charged me a peck, for sure, but that's 'cos he knowed we got money. Same man used ta sell us cattle, and the bugger always upcharged my grandfather."

Sary found it curious: the reference to money. She'd

believed the country offshoots of the Whateleys to be as poor as her own family.

"Never thought much'a Zech; dun't matter he's blood. Lotta the Whateleys en't no good, 'specially's after the way they treat my grandfather. Thiefs, liars, the bunch of 'em. But when I espied me that thar desk, I took a fancy to it, so's I say what the hey, I buyed it." Wilbur frowned in a half-smiling way. "Wun't surprised when Zech charge me *extra* fer takin' it to the tool-haouse in his wagon."

Zech? Sary wondered. "Oh, you mean Zechariah," and instantly Sary's spirits darkened. "I dun't think mutch'a him neither, nor his son Curtis. One time...," but then her revelation dwindled. Why tell Wilbur something so unpleasant? The fact was, Zechariah and Curtis had once paid her a dime each to partake in intercourse with her near the old collapsed Hoadley house, but when their semen had been drained, they'd then seen fit to drain their *bladders* as well, all over her till she was sopping. Many customers, in fact, had felt obliged to urinate on her in her professional past, an impulse she never understood. "They's talk mean ta me fer no reason," she said instead, "so I say ta Hades with 'em."

Wilbur nodded in approval.

"'N fact," she carried on, "I dun't think much'a any of thems that lounge about Obsborn's store. Can tell jess by the way they look in their face they ain't nice folk."

"Naw, most of 'em en't, I'se afraid." The ciphered scribbling continued. "Suthin' 'baout this whole area seem ta be all growed up with bad folk same way a field's growed up with weeds."

Sary rambled on, as she was wont to do when in the midst of someone she liked (which was woefully infrequent). "I went in thar onct ta buy me some rock candy, which be my favorite, but t'was a penny short, and that awful Joe Osborn say he won't give me none unless I fuck 'em all. Over a dang *penny.*"

Wilbur paused again, but looked at her this time in a quelled distress.

"I *didn't,* a'course," Sary added with some haste. "Gawd. I know I got me *some* pride... Then I tried to buy some another time when that old man Tobias Whateley was workin', and I give him a dime but he only give me a nickle's worth."

Suddenly Wilbur was tapping the end of his pen in some remote calculation. "So 'tis rock candy ye like? Wal, I do too." His long arm maneuvered awkwardly until he was able to reach into a pocket. He withdrew a dollar bill. "Seein' haow I'll be writin' a bit more, why dun't you go on up thar'n buy us a big bag?"

Sary thrilled at the prospect and also Wilbur's excess of generosity. *Why's he so nice ta me but en't tried ta git to my pussy?* The instance seemed unfathomable. "Thank yew, Wilbur!" she expressed, jumped up, and took the dollar.

"No point'n ye settin' heer bored whiles I do this—"

"I won't be long!" and she was already directing herself toward the door. "I en't had rock candy is soooo long! Thank yew double!"

Wilbur turned to look at her; his own delight at seeing her so happy appeared muddied by some private distraint.

But Sary knew at a glance. "And *don't worry!* I'll be back!"

Wilbur smiled an interior relief as Sary scurried out the tool-house door.

SIX

July 28, 1928 latur

After Sary wake up, she git all excited wen I give her a dollar for rock candy. Make me feel real good to see her happy like that. She didn't nap atall when I go out earliur, tired as she was, but dozed off after I take off her bandige. Now she be on her way to Osborn's. Few minutes after she leave, I just had to go out to the bush and have at myself with my hand again. Seein her beauty, an just the way she be, and her eyes and smile, leeve me no choice. Saw the pile of my jack-off look disturbed, thogh. Couldnt be a animal on account no critter come neer the house. Hope it weren't Sary who found it and diddled with it—can't imagine what shed think. I probably just mistaken is all.

Was calclating the new Alko passages (I didn't like them at first) I larned as I walked back to the pasture where that fat Rufus boy do all them bad things to Sary. Folks never lern it seems. Also thought hard about what might be wrong with page 751 of the Dee, like exzactly. Cud it be its not the wurds theerselves that was writ in flawed but maybe just the angles of the planes? Frum what I read, the unproper angles would muss up the Dho and the Dho-Hna and make it impossible to send word to the city between the magnetik poles. Just don't know fer sure. Got ta stop worryin and just git reddy.

So anywaye I get back to that old shitty pastureland whitch used to belong ta Elmer Frye, I think, and pick up Hutchins ded collie and sling it over my back. Had to wunder, though, what ole man Hutchins look like on his face (and asettin in that wheelchar I put him in) when his fat son come in all ablubberin and wailin and holding a empty sack that was previous fulla his balls. Bet ole Elam raged shakin his fist and avowin to kill me like he been dewin all these years. I kind of chuckle at the thought cos he know he cant do nuthin to me even if he possess the curage to try. Tis a rule my grandsire teech me long ago when I first started understanding talk, that bad folks don't nevur turn good, they always be bad, and most of em be cowerds too.

But along my walkin root back home, I run into that Kyler fella—who Sary say she never heer of—and he look at me that funny way he look sometimes and kind of smile and tell me, "Aye, Wilbur. Ye be cheerful today, and I am appraised as to why," so I ast him "How ye know why—ah," (and then I smile too), "on account you're a soothsayer, huh?" Then he tell me, "The love ye most seek out with thine heart, ye've already just got. Nay?" Funny thing for him to say. Always like him, and just about him only in this cursed place, but it come to me that he must mean Sary, and theer aint no way he could know bout her being at my place. So I just tell him, "I sure hope so, Kyler, cuz youre right, I am a might cheerfull today and it be on account of a gal." Then he just nod, still smyling. Not once did he ask why I done had one a the Hutchins dogs over my shoulder, neither, and there aint no way he didnt notice. So I bid him a good day but befor I can walk off, he say, "And it mite pleese thee much to know that what it is ye most strive for, ye shall achieve by way of them ancient books ye keep." I stop right then and their and turn bak, knowin full well that what I strive fore most, even more than Sary, is to open the Gate. Wanted tew ask him why he think that but no words cud make their way passed my lips.

Then he say in the end, "Nay, though ye'll not achieve it by the manner in which ye hope most."

And then he nodded with that smile and that was all.

Got me thinkin as I walk back. Like maybe he be a reel soothsayer and not just pretend. And if this be, I don't keer if I kant open the Gate the way I hope long as I open it one way or anothur. But acourse he is likely not a reel fortune sayer.

Walk back double fast to be agin with Sary, even thogh I figure she be sleepin. First, though, I had to feed that One inside so I throw the ded Hutchins dog in the house. Could sense in my brain how close it is all getting and how smart it become. But my biggist worry still be its size, which is why I ben feedin it smaller food. I did the Voorish Sign so to look at it and it seem to have grown mutch since last time. Grandsire were right but the proper time still be far off. Mite have to start feedin it hardly nothing cos I cant ferget my grandsire's dyin'words about how it can't be let to bust quarters afore the night.

Then I fetch what were in the traps and see Sary already out awaitin for me. Made me feel good.

Inside, we talked mutch, and I seed she took a gander at the Dee but I know she wudn't ever be able to understand. If she got religion atall, it be the Christian one. Grandfather always say I should mind my tongue about the Old Ones, so I did. I reckon she had even less lerning than me so how can I spect her to calclate things like what my grandsire call the "Holy Adjudicata and Protocall" bein tampered with purposeful by folks in the past who translayted from other langwiges? When I tell her about how I have to go back to Miskatonic, she say a right smart thing, that sinct Armitage throwed me out that first time, he'd likely do the same a secund, and I got the impression that a stick in the dirt like him wouldnt give me what I want even for alla Grandsire's gold. But I be glad Sary say such, cos it got me thinking bout a better way, and I'm surpized I didn't think on it afore this. But in the name of Him Who Is Not To Be Named, I just HAVE ta git the proper translation of page 751. Ef I don't, like my grandfather warn, it all be no use.

Dang! Whats wrong with me? I ben thinkin so hard about the flaws in that blasted Dee copy, I must uv lost all my sense! Shouldnt never have sent Sary to Obsorns by herself, not aftur she say how they razz her that last time n try to fuck her. I best go there myself right now—

SEVEN

In a manner close to childlike, Sary fairly skipped her way towards Osborn's General Store, which—even when not considering the ignoble character of most of its patrons— was a mercantile establishment she'd never cared for. No negativity, however, wielded the power to vandalize her current disposition, (one which could only be construed as one of unbridled gaiety). Not even the present surroundings could inhibit her; generally, when she traversed the more remote areas (especially those in proximity to Sentinel Hill) she always had her cause for trepidation. The aforesaid hill, for that matter, rose westerly of the path she now scurried along at this precise moment: it and the straggly, rock-strewn meadows fringed by the distant line of unnaturally contorted trees had frequently imparted to her a kind of skulking dread, as though such inanimate things were valuating her with sentient aversion.

Not *this* day, though.

I only juss met Wilbur today and I'se already gettin' good feelin's for him. Ain't never met no one nicer 'n him...

She walked round the rest of Sentinel Hill's brush-hummocked elevation. She whistled a tune—"Yes, We Have No Bananas"—then offered a cheerful wave to a group of overalled denizens lounging higher among a nearby hill's rock-strewn rise. No response was made to her gesture, just blank, decrepit stares, but Sary didn't care. *Why, ya bunch 'a old toads,* she thought. *But I hope yew all have a good day anyways!*

The road—more a trail than a genuine road—straightened through the next meadow, Dunwich Village hulking haggardly in the distance. Sweeps of uncut hay shivered about her, though she perceived not even a wisp of wind. Then...

Is that...a person?

The thing that she first connoted as a bent scarecrow soon turned out to be a person indeed. No apprehension retarded her gait as she proceeded, yet as she did so the figure's details advanced in clarity. A man, shaven-headed, stood beside a lone tree, nearly as if awaiting her. He wore a long-tailed black coat, a white shirt with bow tie, black slacks and leather shoes, but though the apparel clearly had been fine in days agone, they were now quite tattered and threadbare. He stood with the aid of a cane which seemed topped by some flying creature, and though Sary had never been to a moving-picture show, she remembered the time her mother had taken her to Innsmouth on the bus: when the smoke-spewing vehicle had passed through Kingsport it had slowed at an intersection. This pause had given Sary time to glimpse a moving-picture theater, whose marquee had read NOSFERATU and had sported an advertisement poster featuring the quite scary visage whose most salient features were a thin face and bald head, large receded eyes, and cheeks so gaunt they appeared as if in shadow. It was this image she immediately affixed to this waiting person. Closer, she detected the reason for his cane: a severely curvatured spine; then more eccentric facial details came to her heed. Sary possessed no creative alacrity whatever, yet an onlooker who did might describe the man overall as *cadaveresque,* and with a cast of eye (blue eyes they were) that suggested an accursed affinity of misanthropic revelation. At alternate moments he seemed somnambulant, as though not aware of her approach at all, yet other moments he seemed vibrantly notified of all in his range of sight and even beyond. It was then that Sary took note of sinister artwork on his hands and neck, a process she'd heard of called tattooing. Lastly, and most shockingly, the road-stander harbored a metal ring through his nose, akin to the rings implanted to lead cattle or horses.

But when he at last addressed her directly with his foggy blue eyes, his general aspect of negativity evanesced to something rather the opposite. A precipitant smile, in fact, struck her as humanitarian.

In the most archaic Yankee dialect she'd heard in some time, he voiced, "Young gull, greetin's ta ye on this acme of a day. A day of *wonders,* be this, aye?"

Sary considered the uncharacteristic words, then realized the bald man was correct. "Has been for me, yeah." She blinked, remembering Wilbur's mention of a *bald* man. "Say, are yew that Kyler man Wilbur tell me 'bout?"

"'Tis true," the voice creaked in reply. "I espied him not long ago."

"He tell me yew're a *fortune-teller...*"

The man seemed to stand atilt. "Cahn't say I am, cahn't say I en't. But heer's suthin' I *cahn* say: eff'n it's Osborn's whar you be a-headin'..." but then the remainder of the remark retroceded like something lost in smoke.

Sary didn't care for the man's elliptical words, nor in the way his brow cocked; she tried to return a skeptical facial gesture and adjoin it with a similar tone. "Oh, so yew're tellin' me I'm in the way fer a bad time in thar?"

Kyler's head gleamed in the sun. "Mebbe at fust. Thing abaout auguries, like many setch bodements, is they hev a fancy ta change jest as a man's heart cahn change."

"I dun't know what yew're talkin' 'baout," Sary said, amused. She planned to return to her trek forthwith, but the road-stander hastened to add:

"Mebbe I ought come with ye—"

"Naw, no thanks—"

"—while ye be in thar a-fetchin' yew're rock candy. 'Tis of sorts a *devoir* 'a mine—a *duty,* I mean ta say—ta give a jest'n proper *warnin',* so's a man's *heart* hev a chance to *change...*"

Sary had already stopped and turned. It was not the mention of a *warning* which caused her to halt, nor any of what she didn't understand, but instead...

Haow'd he know I'm goin' ta buy rock candy?

The question gave her a motive to add credulity to the man's repute. *'Sides, he a friend of Wilbur's.* "Wal, sure," she invited. "Yew can come along if ya want..."

Very few minutes had elapsed before the duo approached Osborn's. Even with his cane-assisted limp, his pace was difficult for Sary to keep up with. Not once did she catch his eyes straying to her physique, and this was an observation that relieved her.

"Thar it be," he intoned minutes later, but Sary had scarcely heard him, for the sudden launch of a whippoorwill from a brown, desolate stand of bushes gave her a disruptive start.

"Could be a bad omen, could be good," Kyler reflected more under his breath.

Sary dismissed the comment, not quite positive what an omen was. Instead, she watched the queer general store seem to grow twice as large with each forward step—queer inasmuch as it occupied the sagging wood-plank shell of the old Congregational Church which she'd heard had been standing for a long time, since before something called the "Revolution" that took place in a time when men wore three-cornered hats. When the building's looming shadow cloaked them both, even the open air behind them affected an unnaturally darkened hue.

Kyler chuckled waveringly. "Haow's *that* fer a omen?" he said, indicating with his eyes the store's most conspicuous feature: the broken steeple of the House of God this place used to be in days bygone.

Sary twitched at an unanticipated chill but made no reply.

Kyler held the creaking door for her, and they entered

A proverbial cracker barrel sat in the room's front, though Sary had never dared take a cracker—even when making a purchase—since the first time years ago when she'd tried. Tobias, the dismal stick of an old man who tended the counter, had railed, "Get yew're dutty whore hand aout'a them crackers! We dun't care to et nuthin' that's ben touched by hands which's ben corn-fingerin' fellas and jerkin' their dutty peters!" and then one of the Langs—God knew which one, for a plethora of them had been born—swatted the back of her head. In fact, Sary braved an entrance to this drear, shelf-crammed place only when an unavoidable necessity arose. Many of the churlish loafers who frequented the store had done business with Sary, and not one of them had ever offered a kind word, while most had talked her price down, knowing full well the extremes of her poverty.

"Wal, jest *look* what fall off the shit wagon'n roll in my store!" cracked the gaunt, whisker-chinned Tobias.

"Ee-yuh!" the Lang man joined in. "It be the hoo-er!"

"Stew Face!" blurted Henry Wheeler, the fence-post digger whose great belly seemed draped over his belt like a lard-satchel. "And look who be with her! The cripple with the balt head!"

All of the men wore rope belts, hand-stitched boots, and clothes whose blemishes had been constantly corrected by make-shift patches. Stains were rife on these clothes; and had Sary commanded a sense of smell, she might've suspected that the denizens' apparel was washed even less than those who wore it. Amid the cramped room sat a card table bearing several illicit liquor bottles, along with evidence of gambling. In a corner was a typical tin water pail sufficing for a spittoon; Sary took uneasy note that its contents of expectorant was half an inch from overflowing.

Tobias leaned over the counter, his high voice aggravating as an unlubricated caster. "Hey, cripple, why'n't yew clip-clop thet thar cane aout'a heer rut naow, and yorself'n yor whore with it?"

"Ef ye insist," Kyler calmly replied, "but haow much sense be made aout'a runnin' off payin' customers, on accaount I dun't espy much in the way'a *business* heer," and then the man produced a quarter. "A wrap'a licorice is whut I fancy."

Tobias glared, but then resigned. He was as poor as most in these regions; any currency seeking emigration into his proprietorship would not be turned away. Crabbed hands begrudgingly filled a sheet of store paper with said licorice, then wrapped it up.

"Thar's yew're blammed licorice, cripple," Tobias declared, his adam's apple bobbing on his old, thin neck. "Naow git aout."

"Ee-yuh," laughed the girthy Wheeler. "Go'n tell more *fortunes.*"

Kyler tucked his parcel under his arm. "Nay, see, my

friend heer got business as well..."

Tobias and his ramshackle associates all turned hateful glares to Sary.

Even before this, Sary was conscious of assessments being made of her; the hateful glares also possessed more than a small amount of lust as those blood-shot eyes roved her body. One man—the Lang—openly dandled his crotch.

Tobias yelled, waving a bone-thin hand. "Only kind'a business she do is fuckin' and suckin'! She dun't got no cash money!"

"Aw, but I got me some m—" Sary began, yet the owner's outburst would not license the completion of her statement.

"I run a 'spectable operation heer, and I wun't hev no whorin' fer goods!"

Wheeler's brow rose, then he too rubbed his crotch while his eyes narrowed on Sary's form. "Holt on a sec, Tobe. Mebbe we oughta dew some thinkin' on this. Can't hut ta give Stew Face a smidge'a food long as she put a fuckin' on us fust—"

"Ee-yuh," added Lang. Did a tiny spot of wetness darken his crude trousers as his hand continued to knead his genital region? "Jess the look'a this 'un got my pecker *all* riled up. And haow 'baout them tits shewin through thet shiny dress?"

Wheeler nodded with a grin, remarked, "Let's see thet cut on her tew," then briefly raised the hem of Sary's diaphanous gown with a yardstick, the action of which briefly flashed the mound of plush, dark hair between her legs.

Wheeler and Lang whistled.

"Thar some meat fer the dogs!"

"An' my dog's a-barkin'!"

With a half-shriek, Sary jumped at the start, then righted the gown.

This visual treat seemed to ameliorate Tobias' previous condemnation. He, too, caressed his crotch. "Fuh-got jess what a looker she be onct ya git past thet roadkill face..."

"*Thought* yew'd change yer mind, Tobe." Lang made a dismissive laugh. "The pussy on this bitch could put hardwood on a pack'a faggots."

A leering pause caused Sary to shrink; the ill-feeling in her gut gave her a clear impression what was taking place, and it was an impression with which she was all too accustomed. *They dun't even keer that I got money...* By now, erections of various dimensions showed through the pants of the rapists-to-be—even the crackly Tobias, who must've exceeded the age of seventy. "Ee-yuh. Naow's ye all mention it, it been a while sinct my dick had itself a good spit!"

"Any livin' minute this cunt ain't full'a cum be a blammed cryin' shame!"

"And we'll be a-fillin', brother! We'll be a-fillin' it!"

"Gonna get me some shit on my stick too. Mebbe a buttful'a my jism'll make this dutty tramp think twice afore she shew her mess of a face in heer agin!"

Sary was no stranger to such less-than-stately verbal regards, just as she was no stranger to rape. Often, she'd simply resign to it, for resignation tended to minify the physical damage which often played chaperon to resistance. Today, however...

She'd had enough. She made to bolt, but—

"Whar yew goin', gravy boat?" Wheeler's cumbrous form moved with unexpected quickness—right toward Sary—in a manner that left no secret of his intent. The exclamation "Nooo—!" was all poor Sary had time to issue before Wheeler had girded her with his porcine arms. The remainder of her objection was interrupted by the vising of her throat in the crook of the man's elbow; this action produced an immediate reduction of the blood-flow to her brain. Wheeler's other arm wrapped about her abdomen.

Consternation and outrage tried in earnest to break through the force being so brutally administered against her, yet in an instant, her vision dimmed. Her consciousness took on a lolling buoyancy, even as her feet flew off the floor and she was lain roughly on the card table and divorced of her gown...

At once, her body raved.

"It be only fit thet I warn ye," Kyler intoned, yet before he could give more voice—

CLACK!

The Lang man kicked the soothsayer's cane out. Down

Kyler went, to the dusty wood floor.

All I wanted was some rock candy, Sary thought through her fading sentience, *but look what I get instead...* She lay in a torpid daze, and she could see only as if through soiled gauze. As much as she wanted to fight and flee, her muscles made only the most feeble responses to her will. She couldn't move, no, but she could feel, and what she felt was the reality of her physical body being metamorphosed into a smorgasbord of touch-fodder for deviants. Rough hands splayed over her quivering skin, squeezing, kneading, pinching, plucking. Fingers burrowed into her sex, a thumb prodded her anus. Her private hair was stroked adoringly, then abruptly yanked and twisted. Soon it was more than hands she felt molesting her; it was raw, hardening genitals. One penile shaft *pap-pap-papped!* against her lips; another, slicked with spit, was pressed between her breasts and drawn in and out after one of the demented toughs straddled her. A third—Tobias' she would later presume—was squeezed between her feet. Eventually mouths sucked her nipples to numbness; someone may have bitten her inside the thigh.

The visual "gauze" betrayed only the most inchoate blots of darkness, but at least she believed her overall range of vision was ever-so-slowly regaining clarity.

Words seemed echoic.

"This gull's body got my dick jumpin' like bullfrog on a skillet! En't no way better ta get a tickle in yer blood and some feist in her joint like mussin' a whore up jess fer the hell of it!"

"Bet her pussy's had more cock in it than I've had hole cutters in the ever-lovin' *graound!*"

"I'll be a-breakin' my eggs on *these* tits, ee-yuh, but not afore I fuck this pussy like I'se charnin' buttuh!"

When Wheeler pinched her clitoris and twisted, Sary's hips flinched, and she managed to mutter, "Eat shit, fat man..."

Wheeler chortled. "Wal naow, Stew Face, jess fer sayin' that I'll make damn sure *you* be eatin' shit ahf-tuh I'm done tarnin' yer cunt inside-aout with my pecker!"

Cackling exploded; Sary moaned. Her consciousness, indeed, was returning, but she suspected this return would take place only *after* the definitive act of rape had commenced; she knew, likewise, that pleading with the men, or offering them her dollar bill as a dissuasion, would prove a profitless endeavor indeed.

Kyler's voice sounded from a lower angle, surprisingly quiescent. "I warned ye onct, I'll warn ye again, fellas. Yew'll regret whut it be ye're fixin' ta do..."

Wheeler's voice: "Thet balt-headed gimp's pipin' up again."

And Tobias: "Shut yer maouth, cripple, lest ye want it filled with what's in thet spit-can!"

"Mebbe he'd like ta trade thet cane in fer a wheelchar..."

Sary was able to lean slightly up, and found her vision clearing enough to see one blurred shape spreading her legs. Then—

Clunk!

Her head was slammed back down. A now fully hardened penis was seeking entry to her mouth. Sary had recouped enough coherence to yearn, *Gawd, I wish I had my front teeth,* but still could scarcely move. After a pause, the pasty, foreskinned corona pulled back, then fingers dug past her lips. Her mouth was pried open.

"Luke? What'cha fixin' ta dew?"

"Piss in her maouth, a'course."

"Why ya wanna dew thet?"

A chuckle. "Aw, Tobe, thet ain't the question. The question's *why not?*"

Then came a roar of laughter.

The denizen who'd spread her legs was beginning to mount her, when—

"Whut the—" someone huskily exclaimed.

"Hey!"

And Tobias: "Why, yew big butt-ugly shit-smellin' freak!" and then the sound of scuffling. Sary still couldn't see but she could feel that her three molesters had all pulled away.

"Thet witch Levinny's bastert kid!"

Sary received the sense that loud, steady footfalls were making an entrance; then came a *slam!* as a door closed; and at her vision's farther periphery...did something hove into sight? *What's happenin'?* she thought. With a significant effort she was able to lean up on elbows. Why had the men prorogued their carnal fete?

Her vision continued to clear but not enough to discern anything in detail.

"I'se a-fetchin' my gun!"

"Ee-yuh, Tobe. Time someone done away with this buzzard-neck white trash devil."

"Be dewin' justice, mind ye. Ever-one knows it were he who made off with Kelly Bishop!"

"And Lars Low's boy tew! Disappeart last October and en't been seen sinct! "

"And them poor Farr sisters! All they ever faound of them was their blammed *shoes* at the bottom of Sentinel Hill!"

These accusations confused Sary—with some of those names came a ring of familiarity—but something else confused her as well: a *hush* as material as a solid wall that insinuated itself throughout the room. Sary's ears buzzed, while in her mouth an odd mineralish flavor suddenly fizzed. Pricklish static pelted her skin, and she could positively feel her body-hair rising on end from the roots.

Then...

The sound which Sary heard next she could not liken to any manner of aural example in her life. An abstractionist, or an audiologist, or perhaps a hebephrenic writer, might describe it as "guttural pressure," something akin to human utterance yet too distantly departed from the combination of the traversional and longitudinal waves that are referred to as "sound" to be called "vocal." Its source seemed to defy identification, and it would strike the intellectually inclined as a mode of pandemonic transliteration via some sensitivity to a phenomenon with no previously recognized ken.

In truth, though, it was merely the laryngeal vibrations of an only partly terrestrial throat.

These sounds that were not sounds only heightened that queer mineral taste on Sary's palate, while the remonstrances of her attackers had ceased altogether. But as her senses grew more revitalized, her confoundment redoubled.

Exactly *what* was taking place?

At last her vision returned as the blood supply to her brain normalized.

Sary stared.

Alas, Tobias, Lang, and Wheeler were still in the room, but all entertained preposterous poses as their trousers were at their ankles and their genitals not only exposed but so terror-shriveled as to be pathetic. All three ruffians bore the most strained facial expressions, as if in violent resistance against what they were doing...

What they were doing was this:

Lang knelt, his neck inclined forward and his mouth opened wide. It was the suet-white, sack-bellied post-digger Henry Wheeler who stood upright, the withered penis tweezered betwixt thumb and forefinger. Wheeler was urinating unsparingly into the Lang man's mouth, while Lang himself swallowed gulp after gulp after gulp.

But Lang was not the only one consuming a vile substance. Tobias Whateley stood near the corner, his thin forearms shaking as he held in his hands the noxious tin-bucket-turned-spittoon. He'd already raised it to his lips and was—

gulp, gulp, gulp

—swallowing its contents in noisy, grueling increments.

Time seemed to lock in place; the sound of *gulping* held sway over the store. Gulping, gulping, gulping. Eventually, Wheeler's bladder had shed the last of its product, then Lang fell over on his side, curled into a fetal configuration, and began to shiver. But the elderly Tobias...

He just kept on *gulping.*

How much time transpired proved impossible for Sary to take account of, but some considerable time it must've been for it was after only an eternity of staring that the old man finally reached the spit-can's bottom. From his rack-thin frame, however, protruded quite a distended belly, as though a honeydew melon had been slipped beneath his shirt. Then Tobias, too, toppled over, curled up, and convulsed.

When Sary's mortification veered off, she saw that

Edward Lee

Wheeler had already broken from his previous stance and had quite perfunctorily squatted. Amid flatulence that resembled boughs cracking, the post-hole digger moved his bowels directly onto the floor, to deposit a remarkably weighty allotment of excrement.

Why the heck is he...

In spite of the resistant cast of face, Wheeler knelt immediately and began to eat; and it was with no meager zestfulness with which he consumed the self-made meal. When the pile had been transferred entirely into his belly, he licked the floor clean, whereupon, like his cohorts, he sidled over in convulsant misery.

This scene, and the others before it, however, proved *not* to be the strangest that Sary would witness today.

That peculiar sub-aural semi-sound had disintegrated, such that Sary now wondered if she'd heard it at all. Impulse, then, caused her to turn her head...

Wilbur...

Indeed, her surprised gape revealed Wilbur Whateley as the one who'd earlier entered the ramshackle store. The colossally tall man stood as if in trance, mouth open, eyes aimed blankly at the raftered ceiling. Additionally, his hands were outspread, and from each palm issued a modest floret of flame crowned by a smoke-plume which seemed to possess the oddest chlorotic hue. The flame itself, in fact, was possessed of a similar tint. There was something sickish about it. But in the time it took Sary to blink—

The flames and smoke were gone.

Wilbur stood in typical fashion, his gaze addressing Sary. In moments he'd come to her, lifted her off the table, and gently helped her back on with her gown.

"Aw, Sary, I'se so sorry. Dun't know what I was thinkin' lettin' yew come daown heer by yerself—I should'a known these low-daown scum'd pull suthin' like this..."

But Sary felt invigorated. "I'm fine, Wilbur—"

Towering over her, Wilbur gulped. "Did they..."

Sary shook her head with a smile. "Nope. Yew come just in time. Oh, and your friend over theer come in with me."

She scratched her head. "Seemed almost like he knowed them crummy men wouldn't git theer way... Mebbe he *is* a fortune teller."

"Yew mean Kyler?"

"Yeah, he's right th—" but when Sary turned to where the bald man had been knocked down, he was no longer present in the edifice.

She rebuttoned the gown, her mind abounded in perplexity. The three miscreants remained curled on the floor, moaning, twitching, their trousers down. Tobias actually sucked his thumb through his flinches. Sary struggled to refocus on details but found that an overmuch effort was required; her memory took on a haziness that matched her previous faltering vision. *Did I really see what I THINK I saw?*

Wilbur stiffened when Sary innocuously took his hand. Her eyes narrowed in a deep solicitude. "Wilbur, what the heck juss happened? I could'a sweared I saw..." but did she, did she *really?*

Had she *really* seen Lang willingly swallow Wheeler's urine?

Had she *really* seen Tobias consume the spit-can's contents, and Henry Wheeler eat his own feces? And...

Did Wilbur really have FIRE comin' aout his hands?

Wilbur's wedge-like face took on an aspect of desperate mediation. Did his hand tremble slightly in Sary's grasp? "All I done is make them ugly fellas think things they'd otherwise not think."

"Huh?"

"It be hard to 'splain. Ever heer'a *mesmerism?*"

"Wal, no—"

"Haow 'baout hypnosis?"

Sary shook her head. The words meant nothing to her. "Was it-was it...some kind'a *magic* yew was makin'?"

Wilbur's evident nervousness loosened a bit. "Naw, nuthin' like that really, though I can understant why some'd think as sech. Tain't nothin' really but science if ye look hard, jest a way of *distractin'* a man so's ta make him do whut he dun't wanna. I only make him *think* he wanna."

Science? Distraction? Sary wondered. She'd had no proper learning, and knew she possessed little in the way of intelligence, but she was aware of what *those* words meant. *So he made Henry Wheeler THINK he wanna eat his own shit?*

"It be best ye juss not think 'baout it," Wilbur said with a different emphasis, and the emphasis told her this: that somehow, through some means Sary could not cogitate, Wilbur had indeed induced those appalling Dunwichers to debase themselves exactly as she'd seen.

The sudden realization brought upon Sary such a potent sensation of delight that she nearly giggled aloud...

"Let's git aout'a here, afore someone come in," Wilbur suggested. "The state patrol been comin' through Dunwich lately too."

This latter component of Wilbur's information was one that Sary was depressingly aware of. The state patrol had indeed commenced to infrequent patrols of Dunwich since a rash of disappearances had been reported among several of the more remote country-branch families. Sary doubted the efficacy of such patrols, but saw them more as an excuse for the officers to travel off their regular beats and, in a number of cases, threaten to arrest her for vagrancy violations unless she could find in herself a willingness to offer them various sexual gratuities...

"Yeah," she agreed. "Let's go."

Wilbur led her out into the now deepening dusk, but before heading for the road back—

"Wait a sec," he remarked as if something forgotten had just alighted itself. "Whar's that rock candy you come fer?"

Sary bristled. "Them poop-heads in there didn't even give me chance ta buy some 'fore they started messin' with me."

Wilbur went back into the store only to return just as speedily, bearing a five-pound sack of rock candy.

EIGHT

July 29, 1928 midnight

*Was good I got that notion to go to Osborn's cuz just as I
thoght them loafers in there were puttin a hard turn to Sary,
looking to fuck her against her will and whatever else come
inta their dirty heads. But afore they cud have there way, I
did one of the Fire Ensorcellments I learned while saying
the newest Pnakotic stanzas that corresponted with paragraf
1106 on Al Azif like my grandsire taut me to do. It work better
than ever which tells me I'm getting the right intonations. Did
me good to see them men get whats comin to them. Got all
distrakted, though, cuz after she get ma's black gown back on,
Sary take hold my hand. Was reel nice and made me feel like
I never had, had trouble keepin my mind straight. Anyway,
she ast me if it be Magick I pulled on them men but I just
kinda moseed around the topic. Don't know how shed feel if I
told her the whole thing. As for them loafers, I kinda laugh to
myself. Theyll be sick for a few days, but I don't calclate theyll
bother Sary no more.*

    *We walk home, and Sary ask me about the disappearances
cuz she overheard what them men say implyin it was me. I
didnt lie now, I just tell her I didn't take the Farr girls or Lows
boy or that shitty Bishop girl. "Never laid a hand on em," I
tell Sary, and that be true cos it were what I called out the air
that took em, not me. Guess it was a little lie but what cud I
say? She agree anyway that none of em were any good. The
Farr sisters were theeves of the first water, as Grandfather
yewst to say, and the Low boy and Kely Bishop talk bad and
lie bout folks right through there face, me inclooded. I never
call the Old Ones on decent folks but of corse theres not many
good folks round here anyway. "Folk like that be best in the*

bellies of Yog-Sothoths minions," Grandsire say so many times. "En't fit to pick the corn out a my shit."

Was gettin dark by time we get bak to the toolhouse, then Sary and me eat a bunch of rock candy, and I cuold tell she like it a lot. She thank me again for my mother's gown and for helpin her gainst them skell at Obsorns and also the Hutchins boy, and for feedin her and what not, but then I got feeling low when she say to me, "Wal, Wilbur, I guess I better be goin now. I takin up enough of yer time and generosity," so I get all flustered and tell her, "Aint no call to leeve, less acourse ya wanna." She tell me she didnt wanna but was afraid she be incunviencing me, which I assure her she wasnt. "I'd reely like for you to stay," I said but felt funny saying it cuz why wud a beautiful girl like Sary want to stay with me? but she come over and take my hand again, which make me all swoony, and she smiled a sec but then looked down, and say like theres something not right in her heart, "Wilbur, I gotta be honest, and I spect you know already but I don't got no larnin or work skills so...well, I gotta sell myself to men for money. Believe me, I tried but I cant find no other way. Im kind of ashamed but there be nothin else for me." Of corse I already knew this and don't keer so I tell her back "Sary, these are bad times, not jess here but everwhere. Barely any money ta be made. Don't matter what folks do to keep clothes on there back and food in their stomach. Long as it don't hurt no one else, least don't hurt decent folk. Now, when a girl gotta sell herself for money, I don't find nothin wrong with that. My grandfather always tell me it aint good to make judgment about folks, unless we walk in their shoes first." She seem releeved to hear me say this cos I could see by her face that a big burden had been lifted from her tellin me that. Then I say more, "But you don't need to leave here now just ta make money," but I didnt feel I had right to say I didn't like her making money that way. Werent none of my business. But I tell her to wait right there a minute and I go out of the shed and run strait to the little family burying ground with the old iron fence round it. I go direct to the big old flat grave marker stone of my great great great uncle Silas Whateley. On the ash tree which grow right close,

Grandsire had nailed a wood slat cut from the old Hanging Oak used to be in the town square, and on it he carved the words from the Pnakotic which make for what he call a Imperceptibility Conjuration. Now, Silas Whateley's old stone be almost as big as a coffin lid and be heavier than most men hereabouts could lift, and even if they could Grandsire knew they'd never try on account how superstitious Dunwichers be and wouldnt dare meddle inna unconsecrated cemetery— t'would be the worst of luck—and specially since Great Uncle Silas were condemmed by what be calt a Writ of Assize and hanged for sorcery in 1749, and folks round here beleeved to the core of em that if you mess with the grave of a condemmed warlock, you be cursed feirce and all your family too. That is why Grandsire put all the Whateley gold underneeth that big flat marker stone; but he still know he couldn't take no chances. That also be why he put up the Conjuration, cos it make it so anyone who might lift the marker stone wouldnt be able to see the gold in there. First I lift the stone with no trubble since I be stronger n most, and acourse don't see nuthin save for the skeletin of Great Uncle Silas, but then I put my hankerchiff over the words on the wood slat so's to block it out and just like that—that coffin be so fulla coins and gold nuggits Great Uncle's skeletan be almost all covered with it. Also in there, in a metal box, is my own folder I been keepin for yeers, which contain all the most importint pages of the Necronomicon, the Remingius, and the Alko n Eltdown which I translate in to English so whoever come after me won't have a tussle of a time understanding. Plus I also stick in my more recint diary payges not writ in cipher, for the same reason. But anyway I grab a few pieces of gold, then put the stone back to rights and take bak my hankerchiff. Wuz going to go bak to the tool house but stop without thinkin next to the crooked bush. Tis funny how a serious fancy can take a fella over, but see I am so fulla good feelins bout Sary that there I be again goin into the bush to beat myself off, my mind ful of what it be like to make love ta her. Cudnt stop myself, and I dang lost COUNT of how many times I done it just today, and that durn pile of my seed gettin bigger then a cow flop. But I get bak to the shed right qwik give Sary one of the old golden coins and say, "Here be some money so you don't have no need to go do them things with men I spect ya mostly don't like. Itd be a pleasure for you to stay here long as ya want. I wont bother ya none, and ye can go off n do what you want—just be keerful—and I'll be here mostly doin my writing and gettin ready for my next trip to Miskatonic, what I think I already told you about." She stand there sort of funny thinkin and lookin a mite odd at that coin which I guess is worth more n she make in a month of selling herself. She look like she WANT to take it but got to hezzitating, then her shoulders drop down and she tells me, "Wilbur I cant take this money, it wouldn't be right. I already took quite a bit of yor good will, and Im not good with the idea of taking money I havnt erned." "Naw, you just take it cos I don't need it and you do, and be honest I didn't earn it neether, 'twas my grandsires," and then I say she can earn it back by doin chores and such but in trooth I'd never have her do chores, and then I said, "Sides its already dark and there mite be trouble for you ta go walkin home in the dark what with all the scoundrels about," and I got the idea to keep talkin maybe so to change the subject and get her mind offa leevin' and I go on, "By the way, just where is it you live?" She sat back down on the cot, fingering that gold piece, and she tell me to my surprise, "I don't really GOT no place to live now, not for a coupla yeers. I mainly been sleepin under the covered bridges or old basements when the weather's fine, and durin winter, theres some men who—" She stopped splaining but I know that she was gonna say some men who pay ta fuck her let her sleep with them or in their barns or houses and such. Then I just keep on talking to keep her mind distrakted and say "So I take it yer folks don't live round here no more or maybe died like my ma and grandsire?" Kinda bit my lip sayin that, feering that maybe her folks died bad or something and mite mess about her spirits, but she just said like it was nothin how her mother who she loved a lot died a couple uv yeers ago. Twas Doc Houghton who said she was took by her heart seezing up. But her father still live off the old Loveman Trail past Deans Corners, in a log cabin. I remember seeing a log-built cabin just where she say, and since there wasnt others like it on the trale, I figger that must be it, but then I ask "So you don't stay there instead a sleepin under bridges and barns and what not, where its likely to be uncomfortable?" She didn't seem at all bothered answerin, "No, I cud never stay with my pa no more on account of what he been doing to me since I was little." I got all riled deep inside heering that becuz I hear about such things all the time in theese parts, but she just go right on talkin bout it, "yeah, he aint a good man atall. Got to fuckin me when I was real little, like four I guess, and he do it a lot, but then he stop doin that once I get the blood of eve and hair tween my legs, so he make me do him with my mouth instead cos he didnt want me ta get pregnant. Said if he got me pregnant, the baby ud likely be ugly as me and anythin that ugly shudn't live. Yeah, so from then on he'd make do my mouth on his, well, you know, his dick, which he grow to like most of all. Said I did it so good hed make me do it to him four or five times a day, and if I fussed about it, hed wail the tar outa me. Twas him who knock all my front teeth out and he break my nose so many times it got crushed flat and wont never be normal again. Looks like a rotten tomaytuh. Broke my arm once too." She shrug her shoulders then. "Always wonder bout what make people so bad like that. Do you know, Wilbur?" I was itchin with "ire" as my grandfather used to say, from what she say her father do to her, but I try not to show it, and say, "Well, Grandsire tell me many times that some folks is BORN bad and twerent nothin in life that make em that way. 'N fact, he speculated that MOST folks are like that, and its why this world be so frightful. Said most folks are so bad and useless and dishonist and such that they aint fit to be here, that theres other things out theer, I mean like in the universe and such, that got more right ta be here than human folk, and I dare say I think he was right." She look a bit confused by what I said, but then she said back, "Yeah, I know, LOT uv bad folks in these parts, and my pa? He be the worst I ever know. Hes just all sick in his head, I think. One time I member I was about 14 and he make me suck him off but I sed I didnt wanna, so he slap me silly till I cant see straight and next I know he's draggin me out in the woods where he got a big hole dug, big as a grave, it was, so then he tie me up and throwed me in the bottum of that hole and first he pee on me and then you know what he did? He start BURYING me in that hole. He start shovelin' the dirt in yellin' bout how someone ugly as me in the face NEED to be buried just like garbage, and I'm down there cryin' and screaming and he just keep shovelin' in the dirt fixin' to bury me alive but right when he wus just about to cover up my face, he stop and start laughin and tell me he is just jokin, but next time I say I don't want to suck his dick, he'll bury me for reel. So, well, from then on I suck him any time he say without a tiff cos it just aint worth it. Thats how evil that man be—oh, and heres sompthin else. See, when I wuz 17 my ma take me on a trip, only trip I ever been on. She take me near what she call the Big Water to a place called Innsmouth where she got a friend of hers she know since she was a child, and we staid there a whole month, and I cant tell you how nice it twuz to be away from my pa and not gettin hit and not having to suck him. I cried when it was time to go back to the log house, and I even think of running away, but I didn't cos I know my pa wud blame my ma and beat her bad. But anyway when we get back, pa is all outa his wits mad, and first thing he do is lock my ma in the closet, then he drag me to the table ware there's a fruiting jar a-settin, and then he tell me what he done. See, what he done was beat himself off 5 times a day each day I was in Innsmouth, and each time he cum in that jar, then skrew the lid on so his jism don't dry up. THAT's what he done, an I aint zajjerating. 5 TIMES A DAY for the WHOLE MONTH he cum in that jar! By the time ma and me get back, acorse, the jar was more n half filt with his beat off and twas a big jar too. My pa take that lid right off and make me drink it, he did, and he say if I didn't swaller every drop, hed beat my ma and me feerce so, well, I had no choyce, so I drink it, and I tell you it tasted AWFUL it did, worse than normal on account most of it was spoilt. For a whole day I was put up sick with a bellyache like you wudn't believe. And if that wasnt bad enuogh, last summer I think it be, I see him acrost the river pickin cattails, but I knowed he carn't swim so he couldn't come get me, but he yell over that ever sinct I run away from his house, he been savin up all his beat off in jars and one day he'd snatch me and take me back there and make me drink it all and then kill me. Jeez. I thought about that a long time, him makin me do that back then and wantin ta make me do it more, and it just make me hate him so much, but werse was how I got to wonderin about the difference tween bein bad and bein just plane EVIL, cos I knowed full well then that only someone pure EVIL could do somethin like that." She shake her head.

I was boiling up with angur when she got done sayin these things, but what I felt worse than angur was a deep down sadness like I never know before, not just from WHAT she said but HOW she said it, like it didnt bother her at all which I can only figure is cuz shes just so durn used to being treated awful by her father and other folks, that she think being treated awful be just another part of reguler life.

But it AINT just another part of reguler life!

So I decide rite then n there that for all Im worth I gonna prove to her that theers better things in livin than bein treated shitty by folks and being beat and hurt and what not. No sir. What else could she do, bein' a young girl and all? Wasn't nothing SHE could do bout it.

But there sure as SHIT be sumpthin I can do about it.

Im still sitting here at the big desk with the oil lamp turned low, as I'm writin watchin her sleep with the moonlite on her face from the high little window. Every time I look at her, she just seem more beautiful then before, and—

Had ta stop with my pen for a sec cos while I was watchin her she start to turn an toss a bit on the cot, and git ta moanin more then a tad. First I thought it must be a bad dream she be having but then I notice shes kinda smiling and then she gets to rubbin her hands up and down her bodie through my ma's old black dress, and she moan some more louder, then she starts rubbin her bosom with one hand and rubbin her privit place with the other, but I can see she still be asleep. One of her tits fall out the toppa the dress and then she gets to playin with it, and I see the nipple on it grow biggur right before my

79

eyes. *So it become pretty clear to me it aint no bad dream she s havin, it's a good one. Wish I cud believe it was me she was dreemin about but, well, itd be plumb stoopid to think sech a thing.*

Now shes rockin' back and fourth on the cot and really gettin worked up, so mutch that I wudn't be surprised if she wake herself rite up. I will stop writing now, turn the lamp down some more, and watch, an if she wake up I'll act like I fall asleep in my chair—

NINE

It was a rich mixture of feelings with which Sary awakened so abruptly in the middle of the night, and still more such feelings had dominated her cerebrations before she recalled falling asleep. *Them men at Osborn's,* the memory suffused, and then with it the inexplicable delight that she bubbled with upon knowing that her assailants had been forced, by an operandi she failed to understand, to consume horrific substances. She also remained aware of the unusual peaceablility from that point on, since walking back to the tool-house with Wilbur and sharing the rock candy with him. They'd conversed for some time after that, which had pacified her further, but she'd felt slightly uncomfortable when he'd given her the gold piece. Soon, though, Sary's eyelids drooped; she took Wilbur's suggestion to heart, and agreed to stay with him, at least for the night. As awkward as the lengthened cot appeared, she found it comfortable to a luxurious degree; sleep whelmed her in only moments.

She recalled her melange of dreams, then—dreams whose tranquil essentia seemed so inconsonant to her: somnolent images of vast, beauteous pastures whose verdancies filled her spirit with an immeasurable delight; of resplendent and celestial dawns; of grand forests unspoilt by the encroachment of man and his ax for time immemorial, and of the silence of such forests which could only be described as deific. Moreover, partnered with all this, was an all-pervading sense of inner-equitableness the likes of which her heart had never experienced.

What she could not grasp, of course, was the seeming instantaneous *reversal* of the dream's overall mien...

Those beauteous visions of pasture, sky, and wood—quite verily—transposed themselves into a shocking and inscrutable

81

opposite: Osborn's General Store and the trio of nefarious debauchers who'd accosted Sary only hours ago; and it was with her dreaming mind's eye that she gazed at the appalling event. However, as the scene replayed, she found a thoroughly different perspective presented to her: not witnessing the assault as a victim but, this time, as an omnipresent spectator; likewise, it was not via her objective *vision* with which she made her observations but via what one might think of as some manner of hideous *camera dementata...*

Sary saw the perpetrators—and their respective acts of self-degradation—from various flexures and multiple ranges of proximity. One after another, each of them cranked opened their mouth to unwillingly consume the material of their punition. If anything, this ocular recrudescence seemed to take place in a most unnatural *slowness.* Initially, Sary's component of dream-awareness recoiled at the repugnance of this perspective, as would anyone's, yet...

She continued to watch with an undeniable *acceleration* of attentiveness. And what she saw next struck her even more inexplicably:

She saw *herself,* escorted by Wilbur Whateley, leave the derelict general store.

Yet the dream's visuality remained, which enabled her to continue watching, and what she watched would be deemed, by any general canon, as unwatchable.

For a time, the three men had lain shuddering once their stomachs had been filled with unmentionable effluences, and Sary had assumed that the self-inflicted atrocities were at an end.

She was incorrect, however, in this assumption.

It was the age-and wretchedness-wizened Tobias who first came to his feet, doing so in a straining, wincing protestation, as if being puppeteered by a force of will more malignant even than his own; and in jerking motions he picked up the spit-can and began to vomit into it. While this rather noisily ensued, under similar locomotions, Luke Lang and Henry Wheeler each staggered behind the old wood counter, rummaged falteringly amongst the aisles of shelving, and then returned,

Lang bearing a half-gallon glass bottle and Wheeler holding a large bowl. Lang at once girdled the bottle's opening with his lips and began to vomit Wheeler's urine (along with other digestive debris). Into the bowl, of course, Wheeler regurgitated his feces.

Even in the dream-conscience, Sary found no need to ponder over what might next take place...

Tobias passed the spit-can to Lang, Lang passed the urine bottle to Wheeler, and Wheeler passed his heaping bowl to Tobias Whateley, and they all began to consume the contents of these receptacles. Then the process of regurgitation/consumption was repeated, until each man had had the opportunity to sample *all* the offerings of the day.

Sary started awake as if a scream had issued directly into her ear, and with parallel rapidity the dream's constituents appeared in her wakened awareness.

If one could gasp *mentally,* Sary did so, and it was a gasp of fitful wantonness. Her body churned on the mattress, buttocks clenching, toes flexing, sex palpitating. Her fingers were twisting a delicious ache into a gorged nipple, while her other hand seemed determined to admit itself entirely into her womanhood's tender threshold. Her sexual fluids ran rampant; her abdomen sucked in and out as her back stressed like an archer's bow pulled to maximum arciform. In her mind, she knew she was awake, yet that simple acknowledgment is all she seemed able to command. What remained was only a fervent—no—an *inexorable* sexual ravenousness, a yearning for orgasm comparable to the hunger of a donjon convict left unfed for a fortnight. The capability of coherent thought was impossible, overtaken as she was with this raw and primitivistic need to be *penetrated,* to be *cored,* to be drubbed by *immediate* and *interminable* intercourse. In fact, if any analytical thoughts did indeed exist in her head, they were merely recollective images of her dream...

Not the glorious pastures and atavistic sunrises, but her three antagonists cabalistically forced to consume various bodily waste.

She felt aflame, bolting up in the cot. She could hear the

thuds of her heart as her hand bedeviled her sex and her breasts buzzed.

Her eyes snapped wide.

Aw, my GAWD...

The logical queries that such a predicament might bid never arrived, queries that considered her sudden, unquenchable, and very uncharacteristic lust, or, in her own backland dialect, *Haow can dreamin' baout men etting shit 'n drinking pee 'n spit make me so dag blasted horny?* It was a pertinent question, and had Sary been a schooled alienist of, say, the Freudian Doctrine, she might devise that such an excitement came as the result of multiple retrograde symptoms of erotic-reversal revenge totems.

But, lo, Sary was not a schooled alienist.

At any rate, the recollection of nauseating imagery blotted out all else in her mind, leaving only the verisimilitude of sexual appetency and the unheeding drive to slake it.

In labored breaths, she scanned the shed's interior. Only a sliver of light leaked from the oil lamp on the desk, and in this inappreciable illumination, her eyes deciphered the lanky, awkward form of Wilbur, slumped asleep in his chair.

Sary rose as if instigated by Vodou. She walked dizzily to where Wilbur slumbered; then, with no abashment whatever, she skimmed the diaphanous gown over her head and straddled Wilbur bare-groined in the chair. Whether he came awake instantly or not, she had no idea; her focus, instead, had her hands frantic at the man's belt. Several eye-blinks later, his belt was untied, his trousers were opened, and Sary was grunting in an absolutely adamantine effort to haul his trousers down. Wilbur did indeed come awake at this point, and in such a manner as could be likened to outright alarm.

"Suh-Sary! What it be yew're doin', gull?" he exclaimed, and then his hands came to her bare waist, to intercept her efforts.

The words of her reply seemed hewn by the heat of her angst. "Wilbur, I carn't 'splain it at all but I feel jess plumb *out'a my mind* with a hanker ta fuck yew! Got ta thinkin' 'baout all ya done fer me, and 'specially makin' them men do them things at the store and—*jiminee!*—it's got me hornier than a mare in heat!" and with this declaration she was able to jack Wilbur's pants down several inches.

Wilbur hitched them back up. "Aw, no, Sary..."

"Wilbur, please! I dun't know what come over me, but I jess, I juss, I juss GOTTA have yew in me!"

"But-but," and then his large hands finally snapped to her wrists and arrested all movement of her hands. "Thar's suthin' ye dun't understand! See, I'se *different,* is what I'm a-sayin'!"

"*Different?*" she wailed.

"Different from fellas hereabouts!" He broke into an ungovernable stammer. "Different, I mean, duh-duh-duh... *daown thar...*" and then he tremulously gestured his groin.

Utter bafflement contorted Sary's face in the barely visible lamp-light. "Ya mean...yew're *dick?*"

Wilbur froze with the question. "Wal...ee-yuh—"

Sary's tautened wits and sexual delirium had no time for this; her hands shot back to his trouser rivet. Yet his hesitance made fuel for thought: the presumption that he was merely bashful was the first possibility to come to mind (though why should a man as large, physically intimidating, and fearless be bashful?); she also considered that perhaps his genital endowment was less than substantial, an instance which was known to infuse in men no small quantum of insecurity. Either way, though, Sary cared not in the least. She was insatiable— she would have her way, and she would see to it that he did not bemoan the result. "Dun't yew worry abaout nuthin'," shot her scorched-whisper response. "Jess yew *relax* naow an' let me do this!"

At long last, Wilbur resigned to her insistences, but not before turning the lamp all the way down. This Sary took to indicate an embarrassment on his part—again, the Small-Genitals Possibility seemed most probable. Or did he possess some genital *deformity* that he expressly wished her *not* to see? The potential amused her. In the time of her professional calling—and the benefit of knowledge *a posteriori,* one could say—she'd witnessed bifurcated coronae, dual urethras, a trine of testicles, penile shafts bent akin to horseshoes,

85

endomorphic foreskins, and even less cogitable aspects of malconformation. As far as penises were concerned: *I've seen 'em all...*

No, she cared not of Wilbur's unaccountable reservations— *I'm a whore,* she didn't have to remind herself, *and it's a whore's job to make fellas feel good...* Sary determined to do exactly that, but not before making herself feel good as well.

In plenary darkness, she re-opened Wilbur's pants. She was vaguely aware of herself actually *panting* in anticipation of intercourse. Was she drooling as well? Wilbur, however, sat trembling to the bone, as of a puppy ashiver in bitter cold.

His pants were now opened and lowered just enough to grant Sary sufficient access. She could investigate nothing with her eyes but, indeed, her *hands* could investigate, couldn't they?

And investigate they did.

What her fingers reached down and encompassed seemed, forthwith, unrepresentative of the penises she'd experienced, and as for her previous surmise—that Wilbur might be poorly bestowed—this idea held no longer held water. It was a bowed, ax-haft-wide appendage that her grasp had found, which felt tacky and queerly cool. At once, she thought of a fresh plucked goose neck. She ringed her thumb and forefinger, then felt upward to the appendage's terminus. No aggregation of foreskin was discovered, nor was there anything semblant of a glans. It was turgid, yes, as of an erection, yet...did erections lack any manner of a fleshy domed crown? A licked pinky tip, next, examined the more or less stumplike conclusion of the organ, seeking to identify the urethral exit, but...

Thar en't no pee-hole at the end'a his dick!

No. No evidence of any such seminal and urinary aperture.

Nevertheless, and her mystification notwithstanding, with one hand she proceeded to stroke the fleshy but strangely cool shaft, while her other hand delved lower, to cosset his testicles—

No testicles, nor any manner of what might be thought of as a scrotum, could be identified at the shaft's basal root.

Wilbur, she grimly realized, *en't got no nuts...*

86

Instinct impelled her to display no reaction, which came easier, at least, given the stark hardiness of her erotomancy. Unusual or not, Wilbur's genital potential was about to be tested to every limit of thoroughness that Sary could muster. She meant to mount him now, by raising the apex of her thighs high enough to license coitus, and in preparing to do exactly that she opened her hands on his chest to push upward—

As if shocked, she flinched, then froze. Her eyes popped wide in the darkness.

When her opened palms had pressed against his shirt she felt anything but what she'd expected: the rapid squirming of a mass of...*things*...beneath the shirt fabric.

Things? *What* things?

What things could there be that *squirmed* beneath a man's *shirt?* She'd only expected to feel the toned chest muscles of any hard-laboring man, and the indentations of ribs. Instead, Sary had felt something like an aggregation of thin snakes shifting under the fabric. And just as she had flinched, so had Wilbur, as if reacting to the fact of her discovery...

Her lips moved to voice query, but before she could utter as much—

Whoa!

—she flinched once more. One of her hands had lowered most errantly to the inside of his middle-thigh. Here again she felt something quite at odds with what she *should've* felt: something, too, like a snake, only in this case an individual snake much wider than the mass of far more slender things that seemed to wiggle en masse. Might it be a stout rope running down the inside of his pant leg? But that was nonsensical! Why would Wilbur place such a thing there? For a moment she entertained a notion equally ridiculous—that it was not a rope running down his leg at all, but a tail.

But only animals had tails, not men.

Even in the dark, she sensed his alarm. "Wilbur," she began, "what's that yew got under—"

"Shhh," he whispered, and immediately engaged in a distraction potent enough even to quell her questions over such a seeming abnormality. The distraction was simply this:

His middle finger had gently slipped into her vagina, and its entrance brought with it the precursory penetration that she so craved. Gently, yes, but *deeply* as well, for Wilbur's middle finger—she'd noticed shortly after meeting him—extended quite a bit longer than the middle fingers of most men. However, the *extent* of the penetration was not all that bid that initial overwhelming gust of ecstasy; it was also the tactic which was perpetrated. Wilbur deftly churned the finger amid the slippery channel in a configuration similar to a teepee, and this action only aggrandized her pleasures.

Gone, then, was all concern over any physiological incongruities that seemed to present themselves beneath his shirt and down his pant leg.

The most exotic sensations began to spiral upward from the seat of her womanhood, to her breasts and then to her brain. *More,* the thought beat like the very spasms of her groin. *More,* and with this, she raised her pelvis high, grabbed his erection, nudged its tip into her vulva, and—

Ahhhhhhhhhhhhh...

—sat right down on it.

Where Wilbur's finger had catalyzed her to near-frenzy, she now felt skewered and then summarily ushered into libidinal madness, for his genital shaft was double his finger's length. She quivered in place, her nerves thrumming. She could not think in any level of cohesion but could only follow her craven instincts, instincts which demanded she be *plungered* by him. *I need him ta work my pussy like a dang well-pump!* the crude thought swept her.

The workings of the "well-pump," however, would be short-lived.

Wilbur's hips drew back once, then thrust forward, and just when she expected a session of hard, fast, and very deep penetration to commence—

"Aw, aw, Sary!" came the warbled gasp. Wilbur's body went slack beneath her as though he'd collapsed to exhaustion. "I swar, I en't never felt nuthin' so sure-fire *good* in all my life..."

Sary's mouth fell open, and she could've raged. *Fer pity's*

sake! I been with men who come fast, but never THAT fast!
Indeed, the event she'd yearned so torridly for had ended in
less time than it took to begin. A stroke and one-half, perhaps,
of his penis in and out of her, and Wilbur had climaxed. She
couldn't very well berate him—it was his hospitality that had
admitted her here—but still...

*Of all the dag-blasted bum luck! What could be more
mussed up!* She'd been led up to a pinnacle and then thrown
right off into a mire of crushing disappointment. With Wilbur's
failure to engage in coitus for more than a second or two, Sary
felt positively stolen from.

Her shoulders slumped at once. *Oh, well...*

His big hands pressed against her bare hips, urging her off
of his lap. "Dang, Sary," he said almost breathless, "that thar
be the dandiest."

Sary stood up, tongue-tied for a response. All she could
summon was, "Wal, that's good," after which followed the
most awkward pause. She felt silly now, standing there naked,
and not knowing what to do.

This awkwardness, though, ensued for a very short
duration. Sary's curiosity had no choice but to bolster, with
the fact of a very very incontrovertible observation. She was
now standing up; hence, her groin was no longer coupled to
Wilbur's.

She asked herself very slowly, *If I'm over heer, and
Wilbur's over thar...haow come my pussy feels like it still got
a great big dick in it?*

This was quite a momentous question to say the least.

She could still hear his heavy breathing in the almost non-
existent light, and she knew she was standing several feet
away from him now. Could she be mistaken? It didn't seem
possible, yet her conception of logic left her at a loss to do
anything but make certain. She stooped, navigated her hand
to where her sense of proximity told Wilbur to be sitting and,
moreover, to where she believed his crotch was—

There.

There was his thigh, the heavy denim that it was clothed
in more than apparent. Her hand slid higher, then. Had he

already refastened his trousers?

No! Her fingers felt the opened fly.

Then she reached in to feel the evidence of his penis, but—

All her hand came away with was a length of some wet and very sheer film-like substance which, after a lingering inspection with her fingers, she could liken only to a foot-long sausage skin.

An *empty* foot-long sausage skin.

She stood in more bewilderment, blinking in the dark. *What in gad-zooks happened ta his DICK!?* Indeed, her hand should now be holding a limp penis but what it held instead was something she could only ponder of as a limp sleeve—in other words, a sleeve with no arm in it.

And if the "arm" was not in the "sleeve," she made the only deduction she could via the evidence of what she felt between her legs.

Yes, the "arm" was now in her vaginal barrel...

There was no denying the sensation: something long and over an inch thick continued to occupy her vaginal canal, as if she'd been masturbating with, say, a peeled banana yet had inadvertently left the banana in her when the task was done.

Wilbur turned the lamp up slightly, and then appeared as a looming shadow coming to her. His voice resonated in that strange way of his. "Dang, Sary. I know it's more than a fair parcel'a questions ye got. I'll try to my best ta answer 'em," but then, in an abruptness that was at the same time gentle, he picked her up, cradled her in his long arms, and began to step forward, the floorboards creaking.

"But-but whar it be yew're takin' me?"

"Jess the cot, so's ye can have a lie daown. Yew be abaout ta larn one'a the ways I'se different from the other men ye've took up with."

Different? she wanted to protest. *Yew're dang DICK disappeared!*

Something in Wilbur's deportment, however, suggested that *he* knew that *she* knew this, but that she was minding her tongue. The divergences she'd been made apprized of, indeed, obliterated all possibilities of fancy or suggestion.

Her colossal host set her down nude on the cot. "But fer naow, ye're better to jess lay thar. Won't take more'n a speck of time afore ye get yers."

More, more confusion drew lines in Sary's face. "Git my... what?"

"Wal, 'twon't be long 'fore yew yerself'll be comin'..."

Comin'? she wondered. The intercourse was over, that was certain. Did his odd words mean for her to masturbate? Or did—

All ponderment ceased. At once, Sary became intensely aware of sensations beginning to bloom deep in her sex. Although something else remained deep in her sex as well, didn't it? The mysterious *matter* that continued to fill the moist passage as though it were a disconnected erection. And then—

Every nerve in Sary's body began to *hum,* for lack of any other way in which to describe it; and soon she was writhing powerlessly atop the mattress. *Aw, my—aw, my—aw my Gaaaaaaaaaaaaaawd...*

She didn't notice that Wilbur had loped back to his desk, so entrenched she was with this saturation of lewd sensations tremoring out from her sex to her breasts, and then slowly and droolingly spreading about to encapsulate every square inch of her skin. Her sex thumped to the rhythm of her heart; and her breasts thumped similarly. No manner of will could be instigated; only the subconscious commands of her pining sexual instinct. Whatever Wilbur's climax had left burrowed in her vagina, it was reacting in some earthy yet anagogic mystical fashion, piloting her without the benefit of copulation to heights of pleasure thus far unknown, and entreating of her intricacy of nerves every iota of ecstatic potentiality. In moments Sary's quaking spasms girdled the entirety of her body, every muscle clenching in a most concentrated sexual reactivity; and that is when she transcended the primal threshold of orgasm.

But a characteristic orgasm this was not. Instead, the experience first seemed to unroll and then gushingly *explode.* She could've been an erection herself, spasming, spasming, spasming in plush, opiate bliss; she could've been a minuscule bundle of nerves being sucked akin to a gumdrop in a hot, voracious mouth. Indeed, her vagina itself felt as though it were being expertly *sucked* in order to exploit every carnal nerve, while something equally as immaterial seemed to suck out her nipples and lave her skin with the same expertise. Her naked form churned on the bed, helplessly, convulsantly, as she continued to come and come and come, her climax seeming first a distillation of all possible human pleasure, and then an *inundation* of her sexual being. These spasms of flesh-euphoria did not abate after a quibble of seconds as did most orgasms. They did so instead for half an hour.

Upon the experience's fruition, Sary lay in near paralysis: drenched in sweat, eyes rolled back, tongue lolling from an agape mouth. When the most remote traces of cognizance leaked back into her consciousness, she detected very easily that the previous feeling of *stuffed-to-fulness* was no longer present in her vagina. She dopily slipped a hand there for verification, inserted a finger, and found the feminine cavity very wet, very tender, and very absent of obstruction. Her uneducated thoughts then detailed to herself: *I en't never come like that in my whole life!* though what she'd actually undergone was an orgasm precipitated by a para-human constituent. All that her physical investigation divulged of the indicia was a vast region of wetness saturating the sheets between her thighs. She presumed at first that this must be the result of her own womanly fluids escaping during her bliss, but—

There seemed an *awful lot* of such fluids.

She lay like putty amid the sheets, and with some exertion turned her head toward Wilbur, who sat now at his writing desk, looking on with contentment in his dark eyes and strange visage.

Her lips worked to generate speech but the initial attempts failed, leaving her able to only mumble a slew of "blub-blub-blub" noises. The monumental orgasm's remnants had her feeling as though she'd been dipped head to toe into warm vessels full of luscious, alien tinctures whose very contact with human flesh triggered pleasures as potent as they were unearthly. In time, though, she regained more semblance of composure, and was able to chunter: "Holy *jiminee,* Wilbur. Didn't think it were even *possible* ta come like that."

Wilbur's large head nodded in the shadow-diced lamplight. "I knowed yew'd like it, and am glad ye did. Way it 'twas 'splained ta me by my grandsire's that gulls come a mite fierce, and fer longer, on account'a me bein' different from fellas hereabouts."

Fellas hereabouts, the words repeated in her head like stones dropped into hot tar. He'd used that term a number of times, hadn't he? *Yew're different, all right, and I dun't keer none long as yew put a fuckin' like that ta me more 'n onct.*

"And I can tell—like I told ye before—yew got yerself a right pile'a questions 'baout *haow* I'm different, but all's I can best suggest is ye jest leave it be. It en't nuthin' but a bunch's stuff ye likely wouldn't understant anyway."

Sary smiled then, like a sated feline, when she recalled the extent of the pleasures he'd treated her to. "Wilbur, I wun't ask yew *nuthin'* 'baout *nuthin'* 'cos yew gotta sumpin' abaout yew that cud have every woman this side'a Miskatonic River chasin' you like mutts chasin' a meat wagon."

The giant man seemed to fall into a muse just then, as if in some mode of personal rapture. Then he said, "It been a long day had by ye, so yew jess go on ta sleep naow. I'll relax back in my writin' char and ketch me some shut-eye here."

Her response was immediate. "If'n yew sleep in that clunky ole cheer, Wilbur Whateley, I will likely shriek so's ta wake up all the dead aout'a the old buryin' graound, I will."

Wilbur's long, high brow went deep with furrows. "Why... what'cha mean, Sary?"

"Yes sir, I will haowl at the blammed moon...if'n yew dun't come over heer right naow and sleep with me!" and then Sary slid back to afford more room on the cot, and reached her arms out toward Wilbur.

Wilbur rose forthwith, and appeased her supplication.

TEN

Without constraint, however, Sary felt inclined to question Wilbur's obvious intention of coming to bed still donned in all of his clothing, yet an intuition—one formulated in previous observation—at once commanded her to make no such query. Wilbur had already demonstrated some preoccupation anent to his physical aspect, so Sary considered, *Why ask him sumpthin' that he dun't wanna speak of?* No, she mustn't needle him, for fear of imparting a displeasure in his attitude as far as her presence was concerned. She conjectured, instead, that if it were Wilbur's wish to sleep with his clothes on, it was his right as well. But when his awkward frame lowered beside her upon the great cot, he gave voice to several points almost as if he were possessed of a qualification to decrypt her own very concerns while they remained solely with the confines of her mind. Wilbur, sounding drowsy now, said, "Aw, I know theer be lots 'baout me that's got a buzz in ye're bonnet—as my grandsire used to say—and I 'spect that afore, when we was jess gettin' started, ye might'a felt suthin' beneath my shirt, and daown one'a my pant legs, that struck ye as mighty awry, but it be jess like I been sayin'...that not everyone be 'zactly like all folk hereabaouts and what'cha be used to. I'se different, is all, so I don't see that it matters more'n a tittle."

"Oh, it dun't, Wilbur," she was quick in her assurance. "I guess I be a bit nosy sumptimes, 'tis my nature, I guess, 'least my ma used ta say so. So's I'll dew my best not ta rankle ya with silly questions that'd pester ya."

"Aw, naow, dang, Sary," his deep vibrating voice grew lower. "Thar en't nuthin' ye could do ta pester me...," but soon it became apparent to her that the day had stricken Wilbur with a formidable budget of fatigue. *I best juss let him sleep,* her better judgment suggested—though the deferment to her better judgment was quite often not her forte. In fact, even just moments after her monumental orgasm, Sary admitted that another such experience was most notably the object of her desires; and disappointment was not in wait of her.

Again, she was unable to repel this lusty perseverance, and no sooner than Wilbur had begun to snore, she slithered atop him, commenced to abrading her groin to his, and to titillate him with her hands in a most urgent manner. However far removed his penis might be from that of other men, Sary did not now care. She creviced one hand beneath her bare belly in order to re-arouse him, but even upon the instant, a foot-long cylinder of turgidity was effortlessly discerned at his crotch. Her breath felt hot as fish broth, and she whined, "Wilbur, I dun't mean ta disturb yew but—"

The behemothic man did not need to be coaxed further; in fact he seemed just as fidgety for intercourse as she. His huge hands slipped downward, unfastened his trousers, and extracted the sought-after member...

Their previous coupling was reprised posthaste, and ensued correspondingly. Panting, short of breath, and nearly teary-eyed in anticipation, Sary straddled Wilbur and again impaled herself upon the bizarre, rootlike shaft; and after two or three pelvic strokes, her bedmate was seized by ecstatic convulsions. After several moments came a gasp on his part, as his climactic tensions all ran out of him. But now Sary's curiosity thrummed as intently as her craving for more release. That deep fullness was indeed present again in the channel of her sex...

Even after she unstraddled him and left no doubt that genital congress had been cessated. Wilbur's voice croaked, "Aw, honey, that thar was sooooo good..." A moment later, he was asleep.

Sary promptly lay back on her side of the cot. First she let her hand inspect the area just within Wilbur's opened trousers and, unequivocally, her surprising observation of before was repeated. The erection, like a long, raw, and oddly cool pork loin could no longer be found anywhere amid the man's groinal region; instead, only a sheer film-like length of...

something...had seemed to replace it. Again, Sary's "empty sausage skin" simile came to mind. Ludicrously, she wondered even if Wilbur's erection had *separated* itself from his body upon climax, to remain sheathed in her sex, only to *re-grow* for a future copulative opportunity. But this supposition was too outre to take with any sober regard. Hence, a logical conclusion to the conundrum remained to be speculated, and the question had no choice but to coruscate: *What*, in the name of all notions analogous to Sary's conception of normality, could explain the undeniable material breadth that now existed in her vagina?

Next, she felt about her own private region, admitted a finger, and—

What's IN thar?

For something surely was, and the object seemed to parallel quite closely the dimensions of Wilbur's erection. In fact, the substance's morphology indicated that, with the proper level of adroitness, she might even be able to extract it.

Sary finessed her fingers in a way that such an extraction might be made—

But that is when time ran out.

She was at once stolen away on the rushing tide of another sexual culmination. Her body clenched and quaked, her sex seeming to open and close akin to the mouth of a fish out of water. So *infused* she felt with such impossible sensations, it seemed as though some capacity of her brain had entered into arcane collusion with her sex, to unloose the most dense, heady, and intoxicating spasms of uninterrupted carnal delight. She churned mindless atop the cot, grinning lewdly, licking her lips and molesting her breasts, and even shrieking and giggling aloud as she drooled through one bacchanalic fusillade of bliss after another. The experience throbbed on for no less than thirty minutes' time.

How long afterward she lay stupefied, immobile, and incapable of thought could not be estimated. Even after the orgasmic avalanche, she twitched there on the cot in some raw-flesh *denouement* of pulsing nerve-reactivity. More unconscious than sentient this time, her hand feebled to her exploited sexual portal to verify what she already presumed: the "fullness" within had changed to flux, leaving another great splotch of sopping moisture in the sheets. Whatever the object had been, it almost seemed as though the rigors of her orgasm had caused it to liquesce during the relentless contractions.

And Sary felt liquesced herself; the experience had left her like some *thing* that had melted to semi-solidity. It was long before she could move, so all-consuming that second orgasm had been—if anything double the potency of the first. *I gotta have this, like, ALL THE TIME,* her mind squeezed out the greedy thought. Through one of the little windows, the moon glowed, admitting a bandeau of ghostly light. The black patch of her pubic hair shimmered tinsel-like, while the cream-white skin of her belly appeared burnished with oil. Wilbur snored quite resonantly beside her.

Later, Sary found she could move and even teeteringly rise from the cot. She warned herself to be cautious so not to waken Wilbur even before she acknowledged to herself what it was she meant to do. *The lantern,* she thought, and she'd manoeuvered herself off the cot with the utmost gingerness. Her bare feet touched the wood floor, then in a calculated slowness, she padded to the looming desk where the oil lamp remained, turned so low as to emit nearly nothing in the way of illumination. The moon's gossamer radiance alone would not suffice; Sary, ever-so-incrementally, eased the wick up until there existed enough luminescence to make a more detailed scrutiny yet not so much as to breach Wilbur's slumber...

She crept back to the cot, Wilbur's side this time.

It was not the expected empty "sausage skin" that awaited Sary's next delve of hand, but instead...

Another erection.

I juss dun't get what's goin' on...

It was indubitable: Wilbur was different, all right, and given the utter numerousness of patrons Sary's profession had convoked, she was unable to deny his unique genital exclusivity. *What a WEIRD dick it be he's got on him,* her muse put it another way. The organ seemed to vanish after climax

97

and then undergo a momentaneous rematerialization. Like her sausage skin notion, another absurd metaphor occurred to her: a stocking'd foot and then suddenly the foot no longer occupied it...but then a short time later, a *new* foot appeared within. What could explain this?

Closer attention seemed in order.

Sary had been informed, on a myriad of occasions, that one act she possessed an efficacious proclivity for was the act of fellatio; and it was this act, then, that she began to perform upon Wilbur. But so not to wake him, she implemented great care in not jostling him in any way, and not touching him other than with her mouth; and a slow and very dainty process it was. Back and forth her head went, sliding her wet, skilled lips up and down over the queer, foot-long shaft; this adroit action did not persist for long, however, before—

Sary lurched backward in an amount of time far less than it would take for her brain to register alarm and dismay. It seemed as though Wilbur's formidable erection had somehow come *detached* and then *launched* itself into Sary's mouth with more than a little force. Her eyes crossed in the shock of it, yet she remained at least subconsciously apprehensive of the need *not* to awaken her mysterious host; somehow she managed to avoid clunking to the floor from the force of the genitally derived *thing* now jammed in her mouth. As well, she governed herself enough not to gag, as much as she felt inclined, for the object had not only invaded her mouth but also had pushed deep down her throat. The first impulse was to swallow it whole so not to choke...but if she did so, she'd never divulge the object's exact nature. Instead, she trembled, affecting a "crab position," and was able to circumvent what would surely have been a very loud hacking noise. She steeled herself, and slowly and concentratedly forced the bizarre intrusion back out of her throat and onto her bare belly.

It made a wet *pap!* of a noise.

Thank Gawd... Her senses refreshed themselves, and she detected with relief that her shock and her reactive effectuation had not roused Wilbur. The dim lamplight revealed him still inclined on the cot; although when Sary leaned upward and squinted, she saw not a sign of Wilbur's abundant penis but instead just a foot-long squiggle of tissue. But this she noticed via a glimpse, for her attentions had already been drastically diverted by the weighty presence of that which now lay on her belly.

Sary picked the unknown object up in a hand whilst silently manipulating herself to a position by which she could make a more comfortable analysis...

This analysis took but a moment.

Her eyes, now well-accustomed to the scant illumination, fairly *bulged* in their ocular cavities. Yes, the object that Wilbur's member had ejected...was a manner of substance that happenstance had already introduced her to.

Them...thiiiiiiiiiiiiiiiings...

Indeed, Wilbur's penile discharge—obviously the physical matter of his orgasm, just as semen was the physical matter of a more typical man's—she'd confronted earlier in the day, during her exploratory excursion about the property: the pile of lumpen, off-white things deposited in the crook of the drakeberry bush. *Them weird ball-things,* she remembered, *like string 'a white meatballs. They done come aout 'a Wilbur's dick—they 'se his CUM!* Sary could not possibly cognize ejaculant existing so bizarrely and out-of-aspect from what she'd come to regard as normal, but at least this discovery answered a great deal of her questions all at once, and this she delimitated in her own manner of bucolic discernment: *Wilbur's dick en't nothin' but a flimsy sheath, like a sausage skin, which fill up with these meatball things ever time he gets horny. And when he gets his nut, them white meatballs slide aout 'a the sheath!*

The revelation, which was likely to revolt most women, had no such effect on Sary. Instead? She felt quite the opposite: *fascinated.*

Sary of course was not at all familiar with the tenets of Aristotlian Syllogism and its sequent components of deduction by means of axiomatic inference, but she *was* able to deduce this: with a typical man, female orgasm was generally effected through the physical action of copulation, i.e., the repeated insertion and withdrawal of an erect penis within the confines of the vagina; but as Wilbur was clearly *not* a typical man, female orgasm seemed triggered by merely the *presence* of his solid ejaculant in the woman's reproductive orifice. And such orgasms...

Better 'n anything I ever thunk possible...

Sary immediately loaded the "meatballs" into her vagina.

It was all she could do not to cry out. No sooner had she manipulated the aggregation of lumps into her sex, she was writhing on the floor in paroxysmal bliss. Her vaginal vault spasmed like the heart ventricle of a hypertensive cardiac patient; and as if lying in a pool of electrified water, she convulsed time and time and time again, each convulsion eliciting quakes of incalculable pleasure which seemed to defy human sexual capacity.

Half an hour later, she twitched limp on the floor, her face contorted by the most lubricious of grins. More relief surged through her upon noticing that Wilbur was quite a sound sleeper; he'd snored through the entire machination. Part of her scrupled to return to bed before her luck departed, but it was a much greater segment of her that propelled her very quietly forward. At the door, she took considerable heed in pressing up the iron latch, opening the door, and then closing it behind her—all without begetting so much as the tiniest sound.

The warm, star-ridden night sprawled above; the moonlight *brimmed.* The craving of an opium-eater caused her to run as fast as she might—sweating, flushed pink, and unabashedly nude—directly to the drakeberry bush with the queer passage-like indentation. She collapsed to her knees before the pile of her new-found treasure and, salivating akin to a lunatic, lewdly opened her legs and fed the first string of Wilbur's discarded seed into her "pussy." Only a second of thought explained why the pile was here: *It's his beat-off! He come aout here ta jerk his dick so's no one see him, and leave his nut on the graound! It dun't melt away unless it's in a gal's cunt makin' her cum!* and in the second *after* that Sary was squirming on the grass as she was wracked by yet another concussive, thirty-minute-long Grand-Mal-Seizure-like orgasm; and when this was done, it was into her drooling sex that she fed the *next* lumpen string, and thirty minutes after *that,* the next.

And so on.

By the time she'd utilized the entire deposit of Wilbur's "beat-off," she was but a whimpering form of lax flesh incapable of movement. She lay spread-eagled, a veritable spate of fluid seeping into the ground between her legs. The experience all but drowned her in a vat of unearthly ecstasy that had worn her orgasmic capabilities out as completely as water wrung out of wet clothing through a wringer. All the while, the orgiastic grin never left her face; she simply lay there staring insentiently up at the sky's illimitable void as evening expended itself into dawn.

When Sary's ability to cogitate in a fashion more profound than a slow-dripping leak, she felt a jolt of alarm as the sparkling light of morning bathed her naked body. *I best git myself back in bed afore Wilbur wakes up!* but her energy—after last night's saturnalic extravaganza—was slow to summon. What if Wilbur discovered her out here, laying in the grass, fully naked?

What on earth might she offer in explanation?

Only a moment's passage made the question inert. A crunch of dry weeds, a rustle of the bush, and then a towering shadow.

Oh, nooooooo....

"Whut ye...?" The sun blacked out Wilbur's immense, crooked shadow. His head's angle suggested that he was looking down, seemingly, in a brief confusion: first, spying Sary naked and exhausted. Then he noticed the spot where a pile of his strange semen should be—a spot now vacant.

Sary peeped, "Um, Wilbur—I'm, uh—"

Wilbur's next pause gave Sary a chill of dread, but then the gigantesque figure betrayed a restrained chuckle. "Look like ye've figgered aout fast that it's more ways'n one I'm different from fellas hereabaouts." Was he unnerved upon looking more closely at the spot where he'd deposited the wares of his masturbation? "Kind'a embarrassed, I am..."

Sary ached when she attempted to move. "Wilbur, *I* be the one who's embarrassed! Yew jess ketched me aout heer buck nekit and...wal..." She glanced bashfully to where his sperm had been.

"'Tis good ye made use of it"—another small chuckle— "it en't like I could. I jest meant it's a bit embarrassin' sinct ye know naow I been comin' aout heer to this bush, to have at myself with my hand." Wilbur's broad, oddly angled shoulders shrugged. "I juss carn't help it, 'specially sinct..wal, sinct meetin' yew."

An unrefined remark, yes, but in its unrefinement was only the vehicle of the utmost sincerity. Sary felt a glow in her heart.

Quickly, then, Wilbur bent over and in only a moment had picked her up in his hard, rack-like arms. "I was in a low state I was when I waked up, 'cos I thought ye'd up'n left"; Wilbur's enigmatical face shifted as he smiled. "Carn't tell ye haow happy I be findin' ya aout heer."

Sary put her arms about his chest as he carried her— she *liked* being carried by him—and as she did so she again detected the incongruent element beneath his tightly buttoned shirt. *Does he got ROPES tied abaout him?* she wondered, for that's what it felt like through the fabric which she'd noted earlier. Another question might have struck her as well—do ropes squirm like snakes?—but by now the situation reduced these curiosities to mere trifles. Sary didn't care about Wilbur's physical disconsonances. *He dun't keer 'baout all the ways I'm messed up,* she reminded herself. Instead, she smiled and hugged him as he carried her back to the tool-house.

"Guess ye didn't have ye'reself no sleep atall last night," he presumed.

"Wal...no," she said, stretching luxuriantly in the cradle of his arms.

"Naow ya can." He gently lowered her to the cot. "I got some work ta have at. Jest ye sleep whiles I be gone—er, help ye'reself ta whatever ye want."

She looked up intently. "Whar yew goin'?"

"Jest got me some calls ta make'n some odds'n ends," but this was the extent of Wilbur's specificity.

In spite of Sary's exhaustion, some unnamed urgency livened her. "Wal...haow 'baout I come with yew? I can help—"

"'Preciate the thought," Wilbur terminated the notion posthaste, "but, no, on accaount it be the sart'a work I needs ta tend tew myself. 'Sides, ye surely be tired as a ploughman durin' harvest moon."

As last night, so too this morning: Sary *was* depleted of all energy yet at once the idea of sleep seemed intolerable, and she didn't have to wonder the reason. "Wilbur, I'd prefer it *mutch more* if'n yew'd stay heer with me."

While she'd uttered the declaration, she'd moved her hand—without conscious volition—to her sex.

Wilbur nodded with something like abstract joy and self-congratulations intermingled. "I'll be back not far past the noonday...then we'll take keer'a what be on ye're mind, and believe me, I'm lookin' farward to it—"

Sary didn't know what she'd do if he left without first conducting to her more intercourse. Her sleek naked body tensed on the cot; her nipples beetled as if from anger. Just as she would urge herself forward, to unfix his trouser button, though—

Wilbur, still smiling subtly, whispered this phonetic sequence from the Second Eltdown Translations, "Ssssseerdunnnnmurrrrrikfrantnzzzz," and Sary fell fast asleep on the cot. Her host paused to look upon her, and it was a look founded by much more than primitive lust.

No. It was something whose sophistication and intricacy well transcended that. Then he grabbed his carry bag into which he placed his journal tablet and some other things, gazed once more at Sary's sleeping form, sighed, and then left the tool-house.

ELEVEN

July 29, 1928 late morning

Paid respecks to my ma's grave on account today's I'm pretty sure her berthday. The grave is unmarked of corse, one-tenth of a stade in the woods goin north from a 73 degree angle off the first tree at the Cold Glen Crossroads. Even after all this time, I feel bad bout what happened, specially since my ma was dealt a farely poor rasher by nature. All white skinn and pink eyes that was crooked in her head, her hair even whiter, plus it all stickin up like mine, arms and legs not same lengths and all, and one'a her tits stood up high while the other hang down passed her bellybuttin. She was all mazed in her brain, too, my grandfather say, on account of how most branches uv the Whateleys be corupted by ingrowing on therselfs. Wasnt my ma's fault. Grandsire admittd it were a mistake for him to push the old books on her, she didnt understant em—how cud she? Then that fussbudget Mamie Bishop got to pryin and putting stuff in her head against me and Grandsire. Ma just got worse an worse after Grandsire die, and started actin and talkin like she might try to muss up me opening the Gate to Yog-Sothoth. I lernt well from my grandfather that there werent NOTHING more important than opening to Yog-Sothoth, and anyone who try and get in the way, even if it be a blood rellartive, then that can't be allowed, no sir. Had no choice but ta kill her, specially after I was ordered to direct when the ground got to talkin to me on Sentinel Hill.

Still, it were my mother, and I feel more then a speck low about it.

But nows not the tyme to be thinking low. I got lots to be thankfull four. Last night my dreem come true and I got ta be with Sary. Twas weird how she woke up rite when I thoght she

*might. And whut she woke up with was a serious hankering for
me! Prayze be to Yog-Sothoth! All my feers was for naught!
When she find out how my privits was so unlike everone else,
she didnt care a smidge! And it turnt out Grandsire was right
about the effect my seed have on girls from here. But first I got
real scairt becuz Sary put her hands on my shirt and feel my
tentaclettes shift, and I could see she was taken abak; then Im
pretty sure she feel down my pant leg and feel my prososciduct,
but luck be with me again cos all she did was blink and start to
say something but then she left it be. Didn't bat a eye neither
once she feel my dick and reckon the fact I got no balls like
most fellas. If anything she fuckt me, not the other way round!
She seem reel disapointed when I cum on account it happen
so fast, but it didnt take long afore my seed get to workin on
her privit place. Yes, Grandsire was rite and so was the books.
Looked to me that she was gettin way more than she expecked,
carried on all asquirmin and ashreekin and atremblin for quite
a spell, she come so hard. Made me pleased alot to know I cud
make her feel real good like that, and apparently it put qwite a
hook in her cos she got all over me again once we were in bed,
and then after I go asleep, she sneak outside to the crooked
bush and spend the rest of the night stuffin all my old cum
inta herself. I seen my mother doin the same thing after I larnt
what beatin off was, and she got dang wild about it. She'd git
up in wee hours and I'd peep out my winder and see her run
outside, lay on the ground, and start ta feedin each loop uv my
spent jism into her pussy. Often went nuts with it right then n
there, and sometimes Grandsire'd wake up, look out, and just
shake his head, cos he knowed my ma had found about it by
readin in the special books. Another thing Grandsire say onct
is this: "Willy, when a fella make a splittail cum reel dandy,
then she be changed for life. It make her all skewed in the
head for cummin', and make her dew crazy things ta git it."
I was durn yung when he tell me this, so's I'd could guess
little about what he was talkin of. Now, acorse, I know REEL
well. His wurds would ring true, all right, and I would find
that out, yes sir. Yes, my ma was a horny one, all right. Never
onct been fucked by a man from hereabouts bein how ugly*

she be so's no one had a kindle for her, but Grandsire tell me she sure learnt what cuming was the night on Sentinel Hill when my pa knock her up with me and that Other. After that, she cudnt leave off herself! She'd put all manner uv things up her: eers of corn, kewcumberz, broom ends, gords. One time Grandfather was fixing to make carrot and brown sugar pie so's he need the rolling pin to flat out the dough but couldnt find it nowhere. Sure enuf he ketch my mother in her room buck naykid'n jerkin that pin in an out'a herself. Grandsire hadda mind to trash her but culdn't fer how hard bent over he wuz laughin. Another time, I swar, my ma catched a hognose snake bare-hand, and this be about the fattest snake I ever see, like wide as a reglar fella's forarm, and then she tyed its jaws clozed, slicked it up with sum cowfat, and stick THAT up her pussy, 'tis how hot she was to cum. When that pore snake start ta smotherin, it begin to tussle feerce inside a her, and this just make her like it more, and then she cum like a freight train, as my grandsire used to say. Ma even KEEP the snake a couple days dead so to keep stickin it in herselff. Few times ma even try to make me fuck her when I was little but Grandfather got wise to that right off an put a hard thrashin to her. But all this be before she figgured out she cud make herself cum mutch better by stickin my seed in her pussy after I beat off. She got crazy in the head with it, and maybe thats what is happenin to Sary. I find Sary just after daybreak layin there with her tongue out and huffin like a herd dog that be all runned out. Wanted me to do it to her AGAIN before I leave the shed but I sed one of the Languor spells on her cos—dang!—I was just too weared out after the fuckin she put to me.

I guess what happened tween me and Sary was what my grandfather yewst to call a Right of Passage, one uv them things that got to happen to me bfore I become a full man. "Ye carn't force it, Willy, ye jest gotta let it come to yew in the way the Gods think proper. Ye might be tempted ta force it, but then ye likely be tainted by one'a the fair rooker of curses men of the airth got on 'em. See, boy, yew EN'T one'a them men, but only haff, and the other haff'a ye be a hunnert times more importint'n than fellas hereabouts." I wasnt very old when he *tolt me this, and didn't quite follow him. Then another time I was washin an Grandsire got a good gander at my dick, which werent filt at all with cum just then, just hangin empty but reel long, and he say, "Good God DANG, Willy! Thet be some fierce dick ye got on ya, boy! Dun't be dispirited thet ye got no balls like other fellas cos, see, yer balls is INSIDE. And when ye get a yearnin in yer head for a gull, wal, SHEEEEEEEEEE- it! That pecker on ye'll load up with yer jism like packin a durn blunderbuss, it will, and'll be stickin up hard an long as a hammer handle. Heed me, boy, heed me true. Onct women get a gander at yer dick, some of em'll head for the hills, but thar'll be others thet'll follow ye to the ends 'a the airth fer a fuckin!" I were of the age by then to start gettin them yearnins in my head and was already havin at myself with my hand, but I thougt hard bout what Grandsire say, first about how I cant FORCE my proper becomin a man, but also what he say that day, bout how some girls might reely like bein fuckt by me on account how my seed make em cum so good. I like the idea of that, thinkin maybe the girl would wanna be with me. So I member one day not long after, I was comin down Sentinel Hill just after Candlemas Eve cos I liked all the smells up there, and anywaye, I meet up with this girl comin opposite on the trail tween Frye's pasture and the west woods. This girl looked a rite feisty inner sackcloth skirt cut off so's her bare belly show and a top from a old pink blouse with sleeves tore off holdin in a parcel of bosom that my grandsire would say is "formidable," witch I think is the word he used. He wud also call a bosom the likes of this sumetimes "tits aplenty." She had nipples stickin thru that top like they was pipe ends, and I could tell she had a fare plot a hair between her legs too, cuz so mutch there was of it it was pushin out the front of her skirt. The word Grandsire ud use to descrybe this gal I think wud be "fecund," which I guess means she got a look bout her that get a fellas dick up hard right off. The girl turnt out to be Bonnie Sawyer whose I remember with her brother Jeb used to throw rocks and horse-apples at me when I was little comin my way through the Glen. N Fact I knew what fuckin was back then and how my dick and jism differ from that uv fellas hereabouts due to that self same pair, Bonnie and her brother Jeb, cos sometimes on my walks I see the two a them sneak into the old abandinned Corey stable that hasnt been used sinct alla Corey's horses die from some distemper after Grandfather put that hex on em for dumpin their shit buckets in our yard. I peek over the haff doors and watch them git at each other, Bonnie playin with her bruther's dick till it gets to stickin up and then she take it in her mouth, took his balls inner mouth to, and then shed get on her hands 'n knees and hav him do it to her like a dog. Once he pull out and squirt his jism onner back, and I just thuoght Dang, it aint only his dick that be far differnt from mine but his seed too, just kinda white n snotty! Noothing like mine! Couple uv times Bonnie start yellin back at him over her shoulder sayin how he need to put his dick up the hole where her shit come out, and he do that too, witched she seem to like a lot, and there was another time she suck his dick inner mouth and then beat it off on her chest. "Thet's what pa likes best," she said after she done it. Jeb I heard hung himself by the neck in jail that time he got arrested in Aylesbury for trine to fuck some litle girl, and I just thought that was fine. But that be a wile back but now Bonnie she stop me on that old trail next to Frye's grazeland and she act like she don't rmember me and how she yewst to throw rocks, but I swored she really did know. She bring up a big foney smile and say she'll let me fuck her for twenty cents, and it just happend I had twenty cents in my pocket from what Grandsire give me for helping him knock out the downstair walls the day afore. I had sum fire in me that day, on account I was havin what I think is called "puberty" and I was all antsy to pak my dick inna gal's privit place to see what it feels like, so I give her the twenty cents and pull my trousers down, and she just fly into a fit she did when she see my dick already stickin out and fulla my seed and my pants was low enough that my probosciduct slip out and start reelin about over my head with its mouth openin and closing. Screamed a long while, she did, and then she start to cussin at me fierce sayin such like "My ma and pa was right, yew's one of Lucifer's gargoyles, yew be!" I didnt know what to make a that, no sir. "Be damned ta*

Hell!" she say. "'T'was the DEVIL *thet knocked yer ma up with yew, oh I know, that pink-eyed whore-witch Lavinia, and yer grandpa crazy Wizard Whateley that call him up!" and of all things she take a knife out and come at me with it! I wasnt scairt, I just stepped out the way, but my probosciduct don't follow what be in my mind all the time, so it wrapped about her neck in a blink, and lift her up so she hang to deth just like her brother. When it dropped her I just stare and a mite angree I was cos I wanted bad to fuck her which she offered anyway on account of the twenny cents she ast for, but I cudn't very well stick my dick inner pussy now she was dead. That woud'nt be nattrull, and it ud likely cauze the Old Ones to look upon me wth disfavor. Thats what Grandsire ud say, and I larned qwik to heeed his wurds. But there was something Grandsire DIDNT say, he DIDNT say it be unnattrul to set my EYES on a ded gal, nor beat off on her, so's that be just what I did after I open her top so's ta see her big tits sticking up and pull up that skirt to see all that hair on her split, n fact I hadda beat off TWICE on her, and she werent no good anyway so I didnt think it be what Grandfather would call a Transgression. While I was doin this, thouhg, my probosciduct had already slipped up her pussy and took a shit there, a big one. Wished she be still alive a little at least so to be sensable that shit was goin up her pussy. When it was done, I put in back down my pants and get myself fixed up. I knowed then it were best ta always lissen to what Grandfather say. Its bad to FORCE proper things to come to ye, but good to let the gods BRING em. Praise Azazoth. A course I took bak my twenty cents afore I went on my way.*

Right now Im sitting on one uv the smooth rocks down the slope of Sentinel Hill. I guess the word be "nostalgic," but thats how I felt today fur some reeson. I went up the hill previous to gander the big circle of standin stones. Fascinating how they be all set up in a perfect Rhimes circle with six non-Euclidian angles inside. The place smell mighty rich with Their Odor which be a good sign, and I know if it was closer to a Special Time, the ground would be atalkin without even me sayin a intercession. Then I walk up to the big stone slab which I know

109

was carved from rock not from hereabouts. Acourse, my father werent from hereabouts neether, and this place be wear I was conceeved. Guess thats why I got to feeling nostalgik. I was standin zactly where I come from. When I lefft, I heard the sky rumble like it done so many times almost like words, and I knew the Old Ones were smilin on me.

I knew I had some big thinkin to do but I think it best to leave all that out uv my head for now. Sometimes ya think about things too much and wind up foulin up whats coming. Got to keep my Faith, cos Faith is Trooth and Trooth be Power in the Name of Him Who Is Not To Be Named.

Instead I said me some prayers and kiss the soil and the Altar, then go back down the hill with some fire in my eye.

I knew what it be I hadd to do.

Don't know why but as I was heding for the Corners, somthing told me to walk around the woods by the bridge way. Don't know what wud compel me to do sutch becuase the only thing out that way was Nallers ole potato farm. I never mutch cared fore the Nallers. Was them, Ike and his fat, flat-titted wife Prudence, who filed complaints bout Grandsire with the sheriff in Aylesbury how the cows we bought wasnt seen no more shortly after we buy em. Sheriff didnt do nothing cuz when he come by, Grandfather had already lighted a Obfuscation Candle. Then he put a Tormentus Hex on Nallers wife so to make it so her pussy hurt like it got a thorn branch being yanked back and forth in it for six minutes evry hour from dusk to dawn for a whole moon cycle. Grandfather always kinda laff after that sayin such like "Gee, Willy, why ye think Ike Naller look like he en't slept in a month?" Well, the Nallers never filed no more complaints aganst us. Anyway, I didnt know why I'd wanna walk by their farm, but when I do, what I saw refreshed my memry about some things I heard. Standing rite there in the middle of the field was a barn house the likes of which I never dream. TWICE the size of my house, it was, and all made uv fine timber sealed with bug sap, serius roofin, and two hay lofts. It look dang neer brant-new. Then I member that I herd Ike Naller built hisself a new barn a couple of yeers ago, a reel nice one held together with nails insted uv mortice peggs and *had tar neath the roof shingles so it'll never leak, so this must be it. Reminded me also about how Ike Naller up and died last fall when one of his plow mules head-kicked him, and more reecintly them loafers was jabbering at Osborns when I went in for some whale oil, and they was saying how Prudence Naller was lookin to sell that big fancy barn but acorse there wasnt no one in Dunwich with money. Shure enough, wen I walk up to that big barn I see a For Sale sign out frunt. Were no lie neether, it was a dang nice barn, and likely the first new building to be put up in Dunwich since the old mill and, durn, that were built way back in 1806, I think. I was standing their admirin it when I heer a rustle and a sharp wommin's voyce, "What YEW want? Git offa my land less'n yew want a trespassin charge!" and I turnt and see it was Prudence Naller, looking twyce as fat than the last time I see her all that time ago. "Juss was wunderin' what ye be askin' for yer barn, ma'am," I tell her. She dagger-glared me hard and say, "I'se askin' five hunnert, but for YEW I'll take a thousand! And I know no piss-poor Whateley got THET kinda cash!" Oh, I had the cash all right, but I didn't say so. Guess I let her poison voice and look in the eye git to me, and I wanted so bad ta whip up on her a pussy-hurting spell that'd last the resta her LIFE instead of just a moon cycle, and theer was another one I lerned that could make her tits go all full up with pus and then bust and rot off. Why she talk to me like that? And she kepp on talkin, she did, saying I was a low down bastard witchs son, and my ma was a retart, and we was so poor we hadda eat the cobs after we wipe our asses, and my grandsire was a criminal warlock who shuld'a been burnt at the stake and what not, and then she say, "How your retart dirty mama had YEW was by fuckin a blammed GOAT, Wilbur Whateley, and everyone KNOW thet! Cos that be what yew look like, a GOAT!" I kinda smiled wanting to say Hey yew fat hatchet-face old biddy, my father en't no goat, my father be a GOD, but I didn't of course, and I decided I wun't gonna put no extra pussy-hurtin spell on her neether nor nothing else. She just hateful backwater trash not werth my time and effort, and I walk away. The Old Ones surely spect me to use the wunderfull powers they teech for more than the likes of Prudence Naller.*

111

Better she sit and fester all alone with her fat and her hate and her saggin tits and no money.

Then I got back to hedding to my original bizzniss. Deans Corners wasn't but a half mile walk and the Loveman Trail not five skore cubits past that.

It was a shitty lookin little cabin now that I was seeing it again, or maybe my thoughts was colored by knowin bout sum of the shitty things Sary's father did to her in it. Noticed smoke comin out the smoke pipe so I figgered he must be cookin in there, pole cat probablee judging frum the smell. The doorknoker strike me as qweer, jess a old metal plate showing a face with no mouth nor nose, just two eyes. Ugliest knocker I ever see. First I thought just to push the door open, walk in, and take care of the miscreant, a word Grandsire yewst to say, but then it seemed better that I take off my shirt ferst so to get his blood thick with feer before I kill him. Now my own blood was boiling feerce, so when I take off my shirt my tentaclettes was whippin and churning and squirmin like a mass of twennie blood red coperhead snakes, and their mouths all snapping open showing their liddle needle fangs. I was riled up big to see the look on this fellas face when come I through his door!

But I got it in my mind it be better to sneak in the back rather than bust in. I keep quiet as I can once inside, trine not to step on any uv the trash layin about. Werent much of a cabin, couple rooms, dirt floors mostly covered by old planks, and furniture my Grandfather would have laffed at, so slapped together it was. In the kitchen there was a shelff holding at leest ten fruiting jars, and there werent no fruit in em, no sir. They were full instead of some milky likwid, I remembered what Sary tell me, so I didn't hafta wonder what was in em. I get to thinkin so I take the tops offa those jars and let my rite-side domminent tentaclette suck all the cum out of em. Then I hear kind of a panting noyse I thought, while I was moving through the kitchen past the woodstove. I keep my tentaclettes and prosciduct perfect still so they don't make no ruckus, and then I peak round the edge of the doorway. And, well—

There be Sary's father—a skinny, dirty little rube runt, he looked like, scruff faced and mostly bald—settin in a chair and he was buck naykid sure as I am tall. He sit all tensed up with eyes clozed, one hand pullin on his ballbag like it were a bell rope while beatin off furius with his other hand. Hadda be the funniest thing I ever saw, and oh how I wished Grandsire was still alive to see it! And sure enough settin right by him is a haff full fruitin jar, so I know just what he plan. I wate there hiding behind the doorway on purpose, so to give him enough time, then he grab that jar and just when it look like he was gonna have out with his cum, I step into the room.

He drop that jar right away, and I never figured a man could scream like this one did, more like a sheep being gutted than a terrorfied human being. He take one lookit me with my tentaclettes all abuzzin, and I sware his eyes come half out his head! I guess the man was so clutched up in fear that it keep the blood up his dick so it stay hard, and it is reel funny seein a naykid man scream but, well, for some reeson its EVEN FUNNIER when that naykid man be screamin with a hard dick. Anyway, he keep screemin and then try to run off, but one uv my tentaclettes shoot way out and trip him so he fall flat on his face. I pull my trousers down and let my prosciduct come out, and when he see THAT I thought he would up and die. I sent its node lickety split rite up his ass and take a shit. Was a ample meal I eat last night with Sary and likewise it was an ample shit. Packed it all right up inta the middle of his bowels I guess theyre called. Would like to know what thoughts go threw his head when he realize he been filt up with another man's shit. And filt up he was too cos when my prosciduct get done, that piss-ant skinny reprobate scumm werent skinny no more. Belly stuck out on him like Henry Wheeler! "That's for what ye done ta Sary," I tell him, and when he herd the name his mouth fall open, but then I add, "and so is this," and I sent my dominant tentaclette straight down his throte. His belly then get even more bigger cos my tentaclette done empty all that cum from the jars into his stomach. "Ye be et UP with sickness of the head, mister," I told him, "to make Sary drink your jism, and then save it up all this time sinct she leave, fixin ta make her drink it again. What be WRONG with you?"

Guess he didn't heer me thogh, cos his eyes go all crost and look like he was goin to swound.

But now was tyme to do whut I come for.

My probosciduct wrap round his chest like a snake and then constrikt, and you could heer all his rib bones crack at once. I know I hadda move fast bfore he get all cut up inside and go unconscious and die. I fold him right over, a-pushin his head inta his lap, and, see, with his ribs all broke he could be made to lean over farther than natural, and that's when I say, "I heer ye like ta have yer dick sucked, so's now ye can suck it yourself, and if ye dun't, I'll take the top off that woodstove and put you in alive."

Know what he did then?

Yes, sir, he start to suckin his dick.

I make him do it quite a while, and his crackd ribs be grindin and he's whimpuring fieerce and a-cryin like a liddle gurl. Gave me a good feelin to see such a evil fella doin this to hisself, but I knew I best finish up heer and get back to Sary. I keep his head down tween his legs so he keep suckin, and then I send two of my tentaclettes each into his ears, and they started gnawing through till they get to his brain, and then they start eatin his brain-meat. He be convulsin' about then— dick still in his mouth, mind ye—and finally the tentaclettes eet up enough of his brain that he die.

That make my heart sing, it really did, cos the way I calclate it, there be a no more proper way for a fella like this to die than to die with his own dick in his mouth, a belly full of his own cum, and more of my shit up his backside than his own.

I found a can uv lamp oil and throwed it all around the place and put plenny on him too, then run a line to the kitchen. The wood stove be too hot for me to lay my hand on of corse, but not too hot for my probosciduct cuase Grandsire say there be no heat nor fire from the earth that can hurt it, so it knock the whole woodstove over and the spilt coals catch, and then that line of oil turn to fire and run rite back to Sary's father, and that be that. Not a minnute later, I'm a-walkin through the woods at a leeshurly pace and that shitty little cabin with the shitty little man in it be all ablazin'.

TWELVE

The advent of Sary into Wilbur's life and he into hers unfolded as something essentially domestic, and inaugurated into their psyches a sense of contentedness, joy, and synergism that, to objective onlookers, would have seemed, indeed, marital. The broken pieces of one's life were abstractly reassembled by the influence and even the mere presence of the other. To Wilbur, his personal dreams had come to be, and to Sary, she could scarcely believe that life could take place in such a train of wonder.

Though they never utilized the word, they were, for all intents and purposes, in love, and before them both blossomed all the ingredients of a wonderful life together. It was regrettable, then, that such a life would go on for but five more days. Of this, Sary hadn't an inkling.

Wilbur, on the other hand, was in possession of a fair idea that he would be wise to cherish his time with Sary, for time was as of vapor, or of a bird on a wire.

It needs to be retailed, however, that the pair's newfound domesticity, contentedness, and compatibility ensued along with a veritable *extravaganza* of sexual intercourse.

Though many bridges of dubious safety existed in Dunwich, the one worthy of the most remark was the covered, log-spanned bridge just beyond Dean's Corners. If anything of a "landmark" might be referred to in that sordid little carbuncle of a village, this was it. The bridge extended across a more than meager brook which joined the Miskatonic a mile downstream, just as it canted away from the precipitous Round Mountain. In 1694, before the first incarnation of the bridge had been constructed, the men of the settlement's earliest colonists had poisoned the water with carrion and Paris Green, knowing that said water flowed directly through the camp of the aboriginal Pocumtuck Indians, sickening and/or killing scores of squaws and infants, as the adult male contingent of the tribe was out on the hunt. In 1701, the first bridge was built, the same year that the village's original designation, "New Dunnich," had been changed boldly to *Dunwich,* a more direct reference to a legend-cursed hamlet in south eastern England (which had had a fierce repute for black magic and children gone missing) before it was ordered razed in the late sixteenth century by a Court of the Oyer and Terminer; but the accuracy of this information is open to debate. Another questionable rumor persisted as well (regarding the bridge itself, in fact): that the larch logs which comprised its first crossing platform had come from a not-far-off woodland in which still more of the Pocumtucks had been slaughtered via an ambush perpetrated by the next generation of Dunwich men, in 1719. Several of the comeliest squaws had been abducted, lashed to the trees of this wood, and barbarously tortured (with much attention paid to their sexual parts), such that their screams had traveled with sufficient tenor; hence, the "bait" of the "trap" had been set. When the warriors had embarked on what they perceived as a rescue, the Dunwich militia had been waiting with flintlocks, pitch and torches, and blunderbusses. This massacre had effectuated the extinction of the Pocumtuck tribe in His Majesty's Colony of the Massachusetts-Bay.

The fact that, in after-years, more than a few Dunwichers had hanged themselves from the coupling spikes of the bridge gave further fuel to the legend of its provenance. It was beneath this bridge that the Reverend Abijah Hoadley had performed the town's first Congregational christening, in 1746; and in the same water, a year later, that the reverend himself had been drowned quite protractedly. His body, after much violent molestation, had then been fed to swine by what some regarded as the local "coven," presided over by one Silas Ephriam Whateley, a darkly prominent ancestor to Wilbur, and lineal progenitor of those of the Whateley Clan who would choose occultism, incest, and fervid isolation over Puritan society;

and Lammas Night, Roodmas, and All Hallows Even over Easter, Advent, and the Yule. During the hours of darkness, a fair number of girls, women, and, lo, even a few boys had been raped on the bridge; and more than seldom had been the time when backwater strumpets (such as Sary) had plied the enterprises of their trade, only to receive, as the goes the adage, a bit "more than they bargained for." Persons had been murdered on this bridge as well, by the highwaymen of olden times and occasional transients afflicted by malignancies of the brain. Three men had been gelded on the bridge; and one woman, the wife of a bean farmer named Saltonstall, had been "...confront'd b'fore her, while yet behind, and tooke against her Will unto ye Bridge which be know'd as ye *Deane's Corners Bridge,* and then promptlie and with overmuch Violence *strip'd* of all Garment, and thereby forc'd unto Carnal Knowledge with more than severall Men not recognizable to her; where next, she be held down whilst severall barking curs be brung to this most Hideous Scene which then did procede, likewise, to engage in *Unnaturall Consorte* most offensive to God and Abominable in the uttermost to Scripture, upon much Goading and Urging, whilst ye Divellish Perpetrators did Hoot, and did make Exclamations of Laughter, and did clappe their Hands in Plutonian Glee; whereupon—horrid to convey!—this Pore Woman, devout'd Servant of God, be by Knife divorc'd of her Naturall Bosom and then—Lord, protect us!—scalp'd in ye Manner of ye Savages, (yet *not* by Savages so did she spake), not of any Hair upon ye Crown of her Head but yet of her most *Privat Hair,* which be then Made Away With amid Laughter and Revell worthie of Lucifer ye Morning Star himself," asserted the criminal complaint filed with the Scrivener and Clerk of the High-Sheriff. The victim, whose name was Charity Saltonstall, survived for more than a year after the excruciating crime, well long enough to bear the child wrought by the rape, a female-child who would be given the name Melany. Melany, later at the tender age of thirteen, would step onto the bridge and cut her own throat from one jaw-corner to the other, but only after setting fire to the schoolhouse, in which five of her classmates perished. Her teacher perished as well, a Mr. Peaslee, whom diary entries would posthumously reveal to have been sexually seduced by Melany for several years.

Sundry other mutilations, emasculations, disfigurements, and less precise mayhem had also taken place on or in vicinity to the bridge, most with no motives whatever; and during the times of the witch-panics, a drove of women (most of whom were perfectly innocent) had been first branded with Our Savior's mark upon the bosom and the privates, and then dunked into the rushing water below, urged to confess. Given all of this, the perpetual hearthside whispers of grandams was no wonder: that the bridge and its surrounding wood was ghoulishly and indelibly haunted.

Wilbur, however, harbored no such preposterous beliefs.

But it is more than incidental to point out that his first *kiss* had occurred on that very bridge, and the sensation of Sary's lips pressed so unreservedly to his may have caused him to actually weep. Sary's heart—indeed, her very *spirit*—revolved around Wilbur as surely as the moon revolved around the God's Earth. For the first instance in his life, Wilbur was held with unflinching acceptance, not repugnance; and this seemed more than he could believe. Yet believe it he did, for the young woman's devotion was so plain that its authenticity could not be questioned. Not only his unnatural height, nor his shocking visual aspect, but far more intricate characteristics had been, one way or another, observed by his young paramour. The presence of his twenty tentaclettes beneath his shirt, for example, and the snakelike bulge of his prosociduct running down his left pant leg: these traits had surely come to Sary's notice, just as his unrepresentative genitals and semen had already, yet she shewed no sign of revulsion, shock, or alarm. And now, upon the noontime of July's thirtieth day, they kissed quite heatedly under the bridge's rickety wooden awning, which provided but a few openings to permit the entrance of fresh air. When Sary's tongue delved into Wilbur's mouth, it did not hesitate when it came into contact with his own tongue, which was, in fact, forked. She even moaned when the oral investigation made this discovery, almost as if

Wilbur's atypicalities *enhanced* the moxie of her arousal.

It needs to be established that Wilbur was not, by any stretch of interpretation, intellectually challenged, though most took him to be due to his countrified manner, regional vernacular, and speech impediment. On the contrary, aspects of his paternity very much left him equipped to cogitate the length, breadth, and depth of the geometrical sciences, quantum calculus and its inherent syntactic systems, and, indeed, the furthest reaches of even the most combinatoric mathematical thesis—even to the extent that the likes of Wilhelm Gottfried Leibniz and Sir Isaac Newton would feel wholly inept. Similarly, the giant's powers of intellect could be questioned even less due to the fact that he'd taught himself fluent Latin, Greek, Sanskrit, German (along with many participles no longer in use), multiple provincials of Arabic, and also the Alko, Pnakotic, and Eltdown tongues and several more languages with no cradle to the earth. As he'd grown older, in his own personal journal writings— however brilliantly ciphered via an artificial alphabet of his own invention—he elected to scribe in local dialect, in order to leave a shadow of his personality for any who might follow his reverential footsteps, and he had taken up the rather lazy habit of spelling words incorrectly in his haste, but this was but a quibble. The fact remained: Wilbur Whateley was an uncompromised genius of all objective sciences his calling required.

He was *not* a genius, however, in matters less concrete— creativity, for instance—and of the heady variations of romantic and erotic *tactic* he knew precious little. On this day, though, whilst in the midst of a most pleasurable and affectionate embrace with Sary, the words came to Wilbur's mind, *Wal, durn. Mebbe she want suthin' more than me jess stickin' my dick in her. Wouldn't like it not one bit if'n she start ta git bored with me,* so then as Sary's mouth seemed enthralled by the divergencies of his tongue, he slipped her dress up over her hips, said, "Heer ye go," and hoisted her up so that she sat on his shoulders with her crotch to his face. The musk scent and intricate morphology of her vagina left him vibrant with wonder, and it was then that he commanded his forked tongue to first "side-wind" about the delicate rose-pink flesh of her vulva. In time, he admitted the tongue directly into the lubricated channel within, with no little fascination. A shriek of pleasure and her hands insistently going aclutch in his hair gave Wilbur every assurance that she was not adverse to the ministration. The tine of each "fork" roved independently, effecting sensations with which she'd never been acquainted; and by the manner in which she panted, squirmed, and clenched her thighs, Wilbur estimated that she was approaching the fringe of climax *without* the introduction of his columniform sperm, nor even his penis. It was here wherein Wilbur's understanding of female sexual reactivity transitioned into what could only be called "gray area," but since her gestures in response took on an invariably positive bent, he simply continued to maintain the oral process. Next, he allowed his tongue to extend to its farthest physical limit—several feet—and for the tines to part, which his otherworldliness made possible. One he deployed into a minuscule aperture that must have been her urethra (when it penetrated the duct of her bladder, he found the taste within tangy and fascinating), and the other into the even more minuscule ingress of her cervical canal. The activity seemed to incite in Sary a frenzied rising action which she enjoyed to a point of delirium, but after a time, he felt it necessary to see to that action's propulsive descent. This he achieved first by drawing each tine briskly in an out of their respective apertures, and then withdrawing them altogether in order to command them to assume a corkscrew, all the while engaging them to swell in girth, a facilitation also allowed by his para-earthly anatomy. Soon Sary's vaginal vault was filled to excruciating stringency with the mass of spiriferous coils, which expanded and contracted while simultaneously nudging to and fro. The young woman curled into a shrieking ball about Wilbur's head as her climax commenced, and when said climax was at an end, she could only gasp, cry, and quiver in her elevated place. Nothing pleased Wilbur more than to know that she was pleased.

However, by this point, his own arousal was nearly painstaking, so attracted was he to her. He'd already lowered his trousers which permitted of his probosciduct to rove about in revel; and then he gently raised Sary off his shoulders—his beard aglitter and his mouth full of salty sapidity—only to lower her with great finesse onto his erection.

One thrust inward, and one retraction, and Wilbur went wobbly kneed by the freight of his orgasm, while moments later, Sary went writhing in another of her own, which protracted the opiate spasms for thirty more minutes, this process releasing from the inner covered bridge screeches which must have traveled the whole of the upper Miskatonic Valley.

Wilbur cast nervous glances this way and that, fearing passersby, but when none were in evidence, he began to amble out of the bridge. Though all of his mate's orgasms with him had been very much all-consuming, none had been more so than this. Sary had blacked out, which made it necessary for Wilbur to carry her all the way back to the tool-shed like a limp parcel.

This he was all too pleased to do.

THIRTEEN

Perhaps the incongruent yet very welcome issuance of Sary into the quintessence of Wilbur's existence goaded a change in his aforementioned creative deficit. His deportment with regard to her took quite a passionate and romantic turn. Holding her hand whenever they were out became vital to him, and it seemed just as vital to her. And there was no cessation nor diminishment of the joy which now took possessorship of him. They kissed often, and pursued many other modes of physical affection that were not at all sexual in motive. Wilbur found he delighted in the mere sight of her, the mere vision, be she even just sitting, talking nonchalantly, or engaged in some mundane task. Since their second night together—though they did engage themselves sexually at least three times per evening—they slept as if attached to one another, so persistent was their bond. Each morning they awoke, Sary would gigglingly insist that he come outside with her at once—she wearing not a stitch!—and then proceed to kiss him just as the sun began to rise, and she insisted upon the same at dusk. On a different night—she did not recall which—it was Wilbur who devised that they venture to the center-point of Frye's pasture and, beneath the majesty of the moon and twinkling stars, make fervent love.

Another time, after making love yet again, they were taking a scenic walk down an arbored lane near Billington's Wood. Sary's mood reflected an unvoiced concern, that concern being: *Good Gawd, what am I a-gonna do if I lose Wilbur to some other woman?* The prospect, however paranoic, instilled in her a whirlwind of woeful contemplation, for if she were to lose Wilbur, never again would she experience such staggering delights as she had with him through whatever sexual sleight he'd mastered; similarly, she wouldn't likely meet someone so kind, nor someone not repelled by her facial looks. Wilbur, however, was worried himself by what her cast might signify, but he could only guess. "Suthin' clearly worryin' ye, Sary, and I jest become afeared'a what it might be—"

Sary's expression tightened, and she feigned, "Oh, I'se jest fine, Wilbur! I'se not worryin' a'tall..."

"I be thinkin' that with all this great fuckin' we been doin', mebbe...mebbe ye're worried abaout gettin' made in the way, ya know, in the *mother's* way."

The train of Sary's thoughts snapped like a heavy bough. "Oh, Wilbur! I'ud jest *love* that, I would! I will pump babies aout fer yew as many as I can muster if it be watch'a want!"

Wilbur, with this, saw the lengths of his misinterpretation; and the resultant embarrassment easily showed on his face. "Dang, Sary. I was only goin' ta say that ye *needn't* worry 'baout me gettin' ya pregnant on accaount that I *carn't.*"

"Yew *carn't?*"

"Naw, I'se 'fraid not. See, jess as, uh, sarten parts'a me is different from fellas hereabaouts, so's my seed. Way my seed is, is, wal, it en't possible fer it to make a gull have a baby."

Sary's eyes thinned to slits. "Haow yew know?"

"That big book on my table say so, fer one thing, and from what my Grandfather tell me back when I was jess comin' ta be a man. The word he use—wal, it's likely a word that en't known ta ye—the word he use was *incompatible.* See, my seed be *incompatible* with the wombs of women hereabaouts. Means it wun't work—-my seed, that is."

Sary tried to recite the unusual word to herself, but soon gave up.

Wilbur went on a bit of a ramble. "Ee-yuh, Grandsire tell me, all right, he say 'Willy, onct ye stert carryin' on with gulls—and ye can *bet* yew will—ye en't gonna be able to make any of 'em big in the belly with your child,'" but from this point Wilbur curtailed what remained of his grandfather's earthy monologue, which continued, *Yes, sar, boy, ye can whip aout thet big dick'a yers and ye can fuck all these heer Dunwich jism buckets up one side'a taown and daown the next but ye en't NEVER gonna knock 'em up. Um-hmm, ye can fill 'em with your nut like a baker fill a blammed CANNOLI with cream and theer en't no more chance'a yew puttin' a baby up her cunt as theer be a ANT haulin' a bale'a cotton! It be on accaount thet your cum's INCOMPATIBLE with gulls hereababouts...* Hence, the origin of Wilbur's discovery of the word. "Hope ye en't disappointed, Sary. That jess the way it be with me. Chances'a me makin' a baby with yew...wal, thar en't a chance in a quintillion yeers ta the tenth power."

"*How* many yeers?"

"Quintillion ta—er, wal, jess means a long time."

"Wilbur, whether yew make a baby with me or not, I dun't keer," she beamed, "long as I git ta be with yew!"

So much for that interstitial bit of information.

Upon the languishing of the sun on July's final day, however, Sary seemed to sense a figurative cloud spreading over their personal realm, which threatened to overwhelm her joy unutterably, but why she would muse upon this she could not put a finger on. Wilbur spent more time earlier in the day at his desk, writing, and also consulting other arcane papers in his bureau, as well as some books so antiquated that their very bindings were no longer extant. *De Vermis Mysteriis,* she vaguely made out on one title page, and another: *Le Mot est la Vie.* Wilbur regarded these crumbling tomes as though he were viewing a sick loved one. Yet no decrease was observed in the vibrancy of his attitude toward her—if anything there was an *increase*—but betwixt the layers of his undivided attention, Sary very much perceived the afore remarked cloud—a cloud, for sure, of *worry.* During an earlier segment of the evening, he'd been seen pacing back and forth outside before the big house, wringing his overlarge hands, and once he'd unfastened the door's antique locks and gone inside. Had Sary heard a muffled but gargantuan *snort,* and then something like a plaintive *mewl?* Of this she felt sure as she watched through the tiny window, and then she could declare that the mewl reminded her of a domesticated beast in the throes of suffering, so sadly did this aural emission emanate. Then Wilbur had come out, relocked the door, only to turn with what may have been tears in his eyes and an even more intense cast of concern upon his facial aspect. It was, indeed, an *unbridled* concern, as of one far steeped in a misery of inner-calamity. Sary said not a word when he returned to the tool-house but instead efforted to relieve his unspoken distraint by ministering to his genitals with her mouth. The gesture assuaged him a good deal, but then he regretted that he must leave "fer a spell" to tend to some unspoken-of onus, after which he exited the shed, insisted she lock the door behind him—"None ta worry, but jess a precaution, mind ye"—and loped off in the direction of Sentinel Hill. By now, the man's anguish left Sary quite consternated herself, but though she subdued some of this by—unable now to resist, of course— picking up the odd, palish column of Wilbur's spent seed where she'd left it on the floor, and inserting it into her private channel. This affected another half-hour of sheer, carnal bliss, whose impact required yet another half-hour from which to recover her sensibilities and motor skills alike.

By midnight, Wilbur had not returned.

Nor by two a.m.

The deepness of the night sky lent grim assurance that the carriage clock was to be believed and, therefore, Sary was unable to engage her self-restraint further. Frantic, she dressed, opened the shed-door, and prepared at once to begin a search for Wilbur. But no sooner had she stepped without the confines of the abode...

Her eyes stung ever-so-modestly.

Due to Sary's lack of olfactory reception, she did not smell the smoke which had permeated the property like fog; but even in the moon's luminescence, her eyes could very well detect the haze which informed her that a fire blazed not far off. Then she looked west—

She screeched high and piercingly as a steam-train whistle.

A fire burned indeed, from what appeared to be the very spot she suspected was Wilbur's destination: Sentinel Hill. She could even envision the plume of flame wavering behind those queer columns of standing stones where sat the antediluvian slab whispered of by her late mother. An uproarious fire this was not, yet the nexus of its light seemed more intense than any common forest fire should be; while at times, its crackling radiance very definitely gave off flares of the oddest *green,* akin to tarnished bronze. An academic with an intricate imagination and a proclivity for metaphor might describe this hue as *lucifesque.*

However, the entity of Lucifer had no connexion whatsoever. And next?

The *sounds* came.

It was as though the pandemonium of Babylon's demise, the din of the Mongol Horde, and the cacophony of Tartarus entwined and released at once. Had the earth let loose an *a capella* of screams? Was the ground beneath Sary's feet actually *muttering?* From the black sky's void came a CRACK! so chaotic and ear-splitting, she would've not believed such a sound possible; she could only, in her terror, assume that the heavens had ruptured. The wake of the infernal crack was filled with a sound, though not as deafening, possessed of an even worse consignment of aberration, yet she would later realize it was, though less amplified, a sound that carried some familiarity. It could be likened to the resonance of a massive rock-slide, only a rock-slide that was somehow taking place *underground;* and in conjunction, there came an even more abominable sonic accompaniment, something similar to the sound she recalled when she'd heard one of the Grangus bulls dying at Bowen's farm; they'd said that a bovine grippe afflicted the miserable beast, which Sary took to mean something was amiss with its lungs. What she heard this moment—yet from *beneath the ground she stood on*— was a phlegmatic basso flutter, with a repugnant *wetness* to it, but yet also what seemed to be a pattern of *structure.* She grew sick in place, for she had indeed discerned a less profound version of the same when happening by Sentinel Hill in the past.

It was as though some hellish subterranean entity were endeavoring to *form words,* though they be words from no language she could contemplate. If such an utterance might be illustrated, it would be as thus: "*NGH'NAAAAAA-EEEE-BRLUB-H'YUH-D'NAH-YOGSOTHOTH...*"

Then the sky CRACKED! once more. A windless gust slammed Sary flat upon her back, and as still another CRACK! rocked the firmament, she screamed, presuming that the event her mother had once whispered of, the Day of Dissolution, was at hand.

In the margin of a blink, however—

Sary sat up, staring.

—a perfection of silence held dominion over all.

Sary rose, boggled. Surely an experience of such impact could not have been the product of imagination. But her perplexity was not long to last, as the urgence of her mission returned to her mind: Wilbur.

Her eyes flicked back and upward. Atop Sentinel Hill the fire still burned. She leapt ahead with the dread alarm in her heart, and a prayer in her mind exploded forth: *Please, Gawd! Let it be that Wilbur en't up thar in them flames!*

Sary broke into a hard run—

Only to come to a complete halt.

The figure in the smoke-tinged moonlight coming along the trail was Wilbur.

When previously her screech had been one of fright, she now screeched in exultance. She ran ahead and fully jumped into Wilbur's arms, to hug and kiss him, to latch hold onto him for dear life—indeed, the *celebrate* the fact that he'd come off the fiery hill unharmed.

The giant seemed awestruck by the surprise. "Wal, naow—calm ye daown! Why ye be all a-tremble?"

Still hugging him in utmost desperation, she could only reply in pants, gasps, and fits. "I see the flames burnin' up on Sentinel Hill, and had the awfulest notion that's whar yew went off to!" She burst into outright sobs. "Aw, Wilbur! I was so afeared yew be burnin' right along with them flames!"

"Thar, thar, hon." He let his embrace sooth her. "I be jess perfectly fine, as ye can see. 'Tis true I was up Sentinel Hill, but I made it be that the fire I set couldn't spread nowhere."

"The fire...*yew* set?"

"Eee-yuh," he said in a softer intonation. He gently turned her about, to head back to the tool-house. A perceptive person might've noted a shift in his character as if to mollify any trepidation that Sary entertained. Pronouncing the word "worship" as *waship,* he said, "See, fires be the way some folks worship the gods they'se believe in."

Sary's expression suggested cogitation. "Wal, when my ma took me to church sometimes, they inside all dressed up in theer vestments'd light candles afore the sarvice. Is *that* like what yew mean?"

After a pause, Wilbur replied, "Ee-yuh. Same thing in a manner. And, see, I go up Sentinel Hill on accaount that be to me what charch be for most folks—just that it's a different sort of place to pay tribute to what ye believe in. Not ever-one worship the same, nor on the same days neither." He walked slowly with his arm about her shoulder, and he seemed to take considerable care in the words he selected, as if about to divulge to her some manner of deep, intricate tractate. "Jess as most go to charch on Sunday, and on especial days like Christmas and Easter, there's others, like me, who got a *different* religion, that calls on 'em to worship a *different* god, but mind ye, it en't on Sundays, nor on Easter or Christmas but at night mostly, durin' special times like Lammas, fer instance, which be right naow—"

A familiarity sparked in Sary, which gave her reason to make an active remark. "Oh, I know of Lammas 'cos my ma and me heerd the minister talk abaout it onct, back before my father forbid us to go to church. We'd take a loaf've bread and say prayers over it, then burn it so's the smoke float all the way up to God. If I 'member proper, Lammas was haow we thank God for givin' us the fust harvest."

Wilbur nodded resolutely. "'Tis quite true that Lammas fount its way into Christian thinkin' way back, but actually it be much older'n all that. Same goes fur Candlemas which be knowed as Roodmas 'raound heer, and 'tis the day I was borned, matter'a fact. And the same for *Beltane Eve,* also called the Walpurgis Night, and then also for Eve'a All Saints which used to be called Samhain back in olden days they called *Pagan* times, but naow most think of as Hallowe'en. 'Tis funny haow almost all religions on the airth got some link ta them there special days, but what most dun't cal'clate is there be a *reason* they got ketched up with special power that dun't in no way connect to the Christian God nor the Jewish one, nor what folks far off believe in, Gods knowed as Buddha and Allah and such."

Sary was squinting through the information, which she found interesting in spite of her deficit of understanding. "Yew say there be a *reason* them days is special?"

Another determined nod from Wilbur. "There is, surely, and the reason be this: them days is special 'cos of haow the *stars* be arranged."

Sary stared and blinked. "The *stars?*"

"Ee-yuh," Wilbur's inscrutable voice assured. "The way the stars show theerselfs"—he pronounced the next word with much attentiveness—"cosmologically, which I dun't 'spect ye know abaout. Stars like Aldebaran, and Procyon, and Betelgeuse. Has all ta dew with the angles and the planes of their configgerations. S'where the power come from, see? Aw, wal, ye probably dun't, 'cos it be quite taxin' on one's brain and require yeers of study. Took me quite a spell to have a fair understandin'."

At this point, Sary became utterly dispossessed of any hope of comprehension. She recalled none of such things from the church sermons; but then again, she'd always been subject to a less-than-formidable attention span.

Her pace slowed, and she asked the only thing that then occurred to her: "So...what it be yew got is a god *different* from the Christian God an' the man named Jesus?"

"That's right. *Different* from all that."

"Wal...what be *your* God's name?"

Wilbur's hesitation seemed to grow more complex through each stride, and when he spoke to answer, the reply sounded more akin to regurgitation than speaking:

"Yog-Sothoth."

Sary looked at him. Had she heard something queerly similar just minutes ago, not via Wilbur's voice, but pronounced via the impossible mumbling which seemed sourced underground? As she wondered over this, though, she winced, for something, perhaps a natural spasm, or then again perhaps something more foreboding, supplanted in her head an ache that was brief yet pin-point. "Ain't never heard'a him," she said in a shorter breath. "Yew sure he's a real god and not juss make-believe?"

"He be real, all right. I know it. He answers my prayers... Do *your* god answer yer prayers?"

"Oh, yeah!" came Sary's enthusiastic reply. "He did jess naow as a matter'a fact!"

Wilbur's cast of face indicated intense interest. "Jess naow?"

"Um-hmm. I prayed to Him that He make it be yew warn't burnin' up in that fire, and...heer yew is!"

"Ye dun't say?"

"Oh, yeah," she continued, "and 'member that day jest a few days ago, when Rufus Hutchins was puttin' up quite a hurtin' ta me? I prayed for Jesus to save me, and"—Sary squeezed Wilbur's hand—"and lookit what happen! Jesus sent me *yew!*"

Wilbur nodded via a pretense to appear convinced. In his own mind, however, the colossal man was thinking, *I got me a funny feelin' it 'tweren't Jesus...*

FOURTEEN

August 1, 1928 late morning

Came down from Lammas late lass night, and Sary see me. All out of sorts she wuz, thinkin I got burnt up in the Fires. Its funny how things can go so everlivin good and be so bollixed up at the same tyme. Never heard Them speak so clear to me in the passt, and never afore has the manner of my chants work so perfect. I know it be over all this time that the doodads up in my throat that makes for speaking have got well-prackticed and can reech out to the Old Ones far better than any man who be full human and know the same Rites as me. Grandsire tolt me this wud happen, and durn if he warnt right. But of corse with good news there offen be bad, and this be—as Grandfather used to say, I think—"No 'ception to the rool." Earlier I open the house door and go and see that One inside after making the Voorish, and it has got so big it can't barely fit all the way in there. It know now it be eating too mutch, which be why it got too big, but I know it is my fault this happened. I shud've payd more attention, I didnt calclate things right. I felt so bad looking in there and seeing it so starving and misserable. Makes me think bak to that fella Kyler none too long ago, the soothsayer, n how he said somethin like I'll get whut I want but not in the manner I most hope for. Guess he reely is a soothsayer.

Because I know now I will not be able to open the Gate to Yog-Sothoth.

That One in there know it too.

But there stil be plenty to do. Just cuz I cant open to Yog-Sothoth don't mean someone else can't. Why else wuold the Voices on the Hill say what they said?

So anywaye when I come down last nite and got Sary

131

calmed down, she start askin about what I was doing up there, and I was serious on the spot for a answer. So when I tolt her the Fires and all just be another way of worship, she got to talkin about religion, and askin still more. Hope what I sed made sence to her. Least I can tell she not be like most everyone else round here, harborin hate for someone who look diffrent and have different beleefs.

But now that I think about things deeper, I see all is not lost. Just got to be smart and make the Old Ones proud of me. THAT be how I prove to them I am worthy of the privilige they offer me and my exhalted heritage.

Yes. I will prove it all to them.

Sary seem to beleeve in the Christian God, like so many othurs round here claim to. All my life I hear a saying they got and the saying be this: "God works in missterious ways."

So does Yog-Sothoth.

FIFTEEN

Indeed, in a dearth for phraseology more definitive, Wilbur had been well-afforded not only the situation's seriousness but also its *fact:* that this phase of his life would soon be at an end. Yet the example of his existence had hitherto apprized him equally of this: With every end, there came a beginning. This knowledge—for he was *certain* of it—gladdened him to no small measure.

The remainder of the afternoon of the first of August he thrilled to spend with Sary. They ambled the wild brush near Ten Acre Meadows, crossed through fields of stunning flowers, and kissed in the old lattice-work which fronted the abandoned Hyde Mansion. During the entirety of their walk together, only very few moments transpired when they were not holding hands or touching in some endearing way. Wilbur's consciousness, whenever he was in Sary's proximity, felt expanded as if some arcane and impalpable aspect her life-force allowed for him to experience a mode of happiness that exceeded the limit of his brain's qualification to feel it. He was bursting with joy—

—even in the knowledge that he would likely be dead soon.

These "endearing" intimacies—it should come as no wonder—magnified later in the day into activities far more robust, which provided for Wilbur several instantaneous ejaculations, and for Sary several bouts of half-hour-long orgasms. Wilbur's "seed"—it was now plain to her—proved the vital desideratum for orgasms so potent; in fact, the effect of this oddly shaped material on her libidinal system left her more sexually satisfied than nearly any woman to ever trod upon the earth, since only a handful, in all of human history, had ever experienced intercourse with one as para-worldly as

Wilbur. Afterward, with her face imprinted by what seemed a permanent grin of satiation, Sary lay on the cot like something boneless and absent of all vim, though her groinal nerves still pulsed euphorently in post-orgasmic *ecstasis.* The sky was darkening by the time her senses began to resume a semblance of order, and then her previously orgasm-discombobulated vision focused through inconsiderable lamplight; she found Wilbur bent over attentively at his desk, whereto he'd moved the iron-hinged book. His engrossment was undeniable as he was reading intently; his lips moved in silence as he seemed to recite extracts to himself. Sary wanted to go over there and take an interest in his studies, but the carnal "working over" he'd unleashed left her with not even enough energy to move. Minutes later he closed the book rather gingerly, so not to allow any undue noise to be made; it was clear Wilbur believed her to be asleep and sought not to wake her. So...

Sary made no actions to inform him otherwise: she pretended to be deep in slumber, all the while keeping her eyes closed to slits. His spending the day with her had already diverted so much of his time. She had no right to demand more of it by interrupting him.

But... What was he doing?

To the old carven bureau he moved next, opened a drawer, and appeared to engage in some scrutiny while taking stock of something inside. Did Sary hear a few tiny metallic *clinks!* from within? Wilbur took on an expression of frustrated concern, whereafter he paused, then turned carefully and tiptoed toward the elaborate washing chamber. He'd taken the lamp with him, and set it down on the other side of the apparatus, then very slowly pulled out what he'd referred to earlier as a "privacy curtain." Sary was touched by his modesty but more so by the care he was taking to keep from waking her. Now the meager illumination glowed behind him (while he stood in front of it) shielded by the curtain; this arrangement allowed her to view him only as a silhouette.

Sary watched with attentiveness then, as the silhouette began to disrobe.

She'd known full well that—aside from the disconsonance

of his penis—Wilbur's anatomy existed in an extreme departure from the anatomies of other men. That bulkiness, for instance—an often *oscillating* bulkiness—that she'd noted beneath his shirt, not to mention the single hoselike appearance of some evidently organic object that he kept hidden down his pant leg. In the midst of their intercourse on the covered bridge, Sary even thought she may have detected this object's emergence when Wilbur had lowered his trousers—the impression she'd received was that of a girthy multicolored snake roving independently about as she succumbed to his oral succor and genital penetration. Yet her orgasms had been so propulsive and absolute that she honestly didn't care *what* the bizarre appendage might be. The acknowledgment, in other words, was obvious: Wilbur was physically different from typical men, and this atypicality (for whatever reason might explain it) was immaterial to her. Her only concerns were of Wilbur, and the cruciality that he understood the thoroughgoing manner with which she cared for him. Just at that moment, her eyes rapt on his silhouette, she mused, *Wilbur could be a durn DEMON and I wouldn't keer. Naw, I wouldn't love him no less...*

She saw with no difficulty that Wilbur had removed all his clothing behind the illumined curtain, and, yes, the curious and even writhing *bulk* about his lower chest she saw as well. Likewise, that organic object that ran down his pant leg was now liberated from the confinement of his trousers and, just as she'd thought, it hovered about him as the giant man prepared to wash. This was not the first time Sary would wonder if Wilbur was actually possessed of a *tail.* But as her curiosity heightened so did her arousal; she *needed* him yet again, to experience still more of that sexual cabalism that he and only he could deliver to her; so an idea sparked at once in her mind and she said, "Wilbur?"

The silhouette froze. "Aw, durn, Sary," came the warbled respond. "I'se sorry I waked ye. 'Twas trine hard not tew."

"Naw, I warn't asleep." She giggled. "I'se watchin' yew 'hind that cartin, and a-gettin' mighty hot, if yew know what I mean. Dang, Wilbur, I'se so *'tracted* ta yew, I could jess squeal. And-and, wal, mebbe yew en't of the sart ta wanna heer words from a gal that's *serious*, but I got me no choice but ta say thet yew're jess-jess, like, *reely important* ta me..."

Wilbur's black silhouette remained frozen.

Sary continued, her voice soft and lilting by its enrichment from desire. "I en't never felt so good 'baout a fella as I feel fer yew."

More silence from the wash-cove, perhaps for as much as a full minute. Then Wilbur replied in a strange, stifled half-choke: "And theer en't nuthin' never made me so happy as what ye jest said."

The seriousness of these conveyances seemed to materially thicken the air, like broth converting to roux. Sary knew she mustn't overwhelm him with her feelings now, for they were ultimately selfish, and she knew that much was on his mind of late. So she changed the motive of her words: "Would yew like it if I come in theer with ya and help ya warsh? I'd jess be et up with happy were yew ta let me have my hands all abaout ya."

The bulk surrounding the silhouette's lower chest seemed to shift more actively; and the "tail" moved about with more deliberation. But Wilbur's dark voice said, "Mutch as I'd like ye tew, I'm afeered ye'd be reely disquieted by seein' me full naked. Ye already know that theer be a lot abaout me quite different from fellas as ye're used to—"

"Wilbur!" she exclaimed, "I dun't keer, not one bit!"

"—but, wal, I got me a idea..."

Emotion pulled at Wilbur's *élan vital* as of one whose arms had been lashed to opposing steeds. Wilbur's joy at having been informed of his importance to Sary had nearly caused him to collapse in a tumult of jubilant tears. There'd been nothing of the disingenuous in her voice, nothing at all, while another of Wilbur's otherworldly aptitudes enabled him to detect with some accuracy when one was conveying untruths. Yet the impact of his joy was almost as immediately superceded by a riveting *fear.*

What it be Sary wants right naow is more hobknobbin'

and... He looked down at his penis, which remained an empty sheath.

Not even a specimen as vastly deviated from humankind as Wilbur could successfully engage in intercourse with such rapidity that he might possess an *instantaneous* sexual recovery. *Dang, all this fuckin' we been doin' has up 'n left me limp as a cut-off dog tail;* in other words, intercourse with her just now had been rendered impossible. At once, though, he recalled her seeming ecstasy when he'd tended to her privates with his tongue that day on the bridge. He considered repeating this gesture, but then, a more diverse possibility occurred to him...

"Wilbur?"she insisted. "What's this ideer'a yours?"

The curtain, of course, still intercepted her view of him, but he would need to give up this veil. "All right noaw," he said, "what ye need ta do fust is go'n pull closed all the curtains over the little windows."

Her excited movements were easily overheard as she discharged the instructions and came back to the cot. "I done it. What naow?"

"Naow? Wal, jest ye wait a sec," and then he fully turned down the oil lamp's wick. Darkness filled up the room.

"What can ye see?" he inquired.

"Why, nuthin', a'course! 'Tween the cartins closed and yew puttin' off the lamp, it be darker than the bottom of a rabbit hole!"

"Good," Wilbur murmured. Then, completely naked, he stepped out from behind the privacy curtain and began to approach the cot.

"Wilbur?"

"I'se right heer, hon. I'se comin' over—"

"Wal be keerful yew dun't fall! Haow can ya see?"

"I'se jess fine, Sary," he assured, as he *was* able to see, even in such tenebrousness. It might be appropriate to mention that the eyes in Wilbur's head were essentially as normal as those of typic men; and with them, indeed, he could scarcely see a thing. Yet the paternal side of his genetic inheritance had graced him not only with two eyes in his head but also—

Edward Lee

Two *more* eyes in his hips.

These were described in Hazred's *Al Azif* as "ancillary ocular organs." Did they appear as human eyes as well?

The answer to that would be an indubitable *no.*

The fringe of cilia surrounding each was nothing akin to eyelashes. Instead these protective hair-like strands were motile, greenish-yellow in color, and possessed of collateral sensory nerves. Each eye, too, was harbored at the front of each hip by a cusp of pink, porous mesenteric tissue which existed quite unlike a typical socket of bone. The eyes were oval, not spheric, and black, not white, with only a diminutive aperture to suffice for pupil and iris. With them exposed like this, Wilbur could see acutely through utter lightlessness, heavy fog, and torrential rain and snow; indeed, he could even see through certain solid obstructions such as clothing, wood panels, and none-too-dense sheet metal.

And just now he could, to a great and enthusiastic detail, see Sary as she lay awaiting him on the cot, her naked physique cringing for him, her breasts near to pulsing, and the frenzy of anticipation coning her nipples. She cringed further as she tried but failed to resist the impulse to stimulate her sex manually.

"Aw, Wilbur," came her parched, liquid-like whisper, "all's I'se livin' fer of late is ta be made love to by yew..."

Wilbur stepped ahead, his tentaclettes all aflutter and his prosciduct elevated and pendulating. "Heer I be," his own facsimile of a whisper returned and then he leaned carefully over, visually adoring her body with his rudimentary eyes. "Gonna tetch ye naow, but it'll be differnt from what ye expect."

"Dew it, please, Wilbur! Carn't stand waitin' ta feel ya..."

As has been aforementioned, the area of Wilbur's body that, when juxtaposed to a human's, would be identified as his "thorax" or upper abdomen/lower chest, was outgrown with exactly twenty boneless appendages. These were similar morphologically to, say, common garden snakes: each being possessed of a yard's length (though further extension was possible) and a width of a half an inch. Each, too, possessed

138

a terminus akin to a cephalopodic "sucker" combined with a mouth, and was rimmed by protractible fangs comparable to fishbones in width yet a strength far surpassing any metallic element on the known Periodic Chart. These examples of dentation Wilbur mentally commanded now to retract entirely. Additional mention, however, is thus: only *eighteen* of Wilbur's tentaclettes were as described. Each side of his thorax also possessed one larger and more diverse tentaclette. Wilbur's grandfather had called them the "dominant" tentaclettes, while they were referred to in the Wormius' translation of the *Necronomicon* as the *"tentaculum superiora."*

It was the pair of these organs which Wilbur's mind now summoned to action.

He wielded them slowly and precisely, to adhere their silver-dollar-sized suckers to each of Sary's nipples; each sucker, it has until now been neglected to add, possessed a much smaller sucker within—a sucker within a sucker, in a sense—so that the smaller affixed themselves to each of Sary's papillae, while the more encompassing organ covered the entire areola.

And next, as was their function, they began to *suck*.

The sudden and quite exotic pleasure so immediately generated caused Sary to squirm, tense, and moan just as immediately. Yet this action existed only as the *aperitif* of what Wilbur envisioned. Eighteen more tentaclettes remained to be utilized, and the colossan wasted no time in manipulating the sucker of each to attentively encompass the tender, super-sensitive flesh of Sary's majora and minora, and her clitoral node as well. These, too, began to suck with a steadfast precision. The intricate process, of course, provided for Sary an even more adventive means of pleasure; and the eruption of responses from her sexual nerve-network became plain with the rise of her moans and the extent of her pelvic convulsions. Wilbur, to himself, celebrated his craft in producing such a gratifying stimuli for her.

Still more remained, however.

His prosciduct reared, as if excited itself by the prospect of its next task. This malleable, tail-like appendage could extend to a length of six or so yards, and was fascinatingly adorned by purplish emblems of an annular or spiral nature. And though its terminus was indeed fitted by a fleshy duct capable of ingestion and expulsion, Wilbur's extra-dimensional genes provided it not with teeth. It did, on the other hand, come equipped with an exaggeration of a tongue which, where taste buds would be on a terrestrial tongue, sported hundreds of diminutive wedges, better described as being like *larks'* tongues. Wilbur required no great amount of contemplation as how to most creatively apply these minuscule tubules.

He brought the probosciduct to bear, so to speak, down between his own legs, and not quite but very nearly entering Sary's vagina. The appendage would not seek penetration, but its otherworldly tongue would. With a careful slowness at first, the tongue slid forward, delving to the farthest depth of Sary's vaginal canal, then with the same slowness began to protract and withdraw, all the while (since it was expandable) swelling to a girth which far exceeded that of Wilbur's erection, or the erection in fact of any human male. Simultaneously, of course, the myriad of tiny tubules began to lick, revolve around, and otherwise titillate every square millimeter of Sary's interior vagina.

The process elicited the desired effect, as the young woman flew into a delirium of exhilarating spasmodic reactivity. Wilbur then increased the tempo of the back-and-forth penetrations, until they reached a cycle more akin to that of the piston of a motor than the carnal thrusts of a man. Meanwhile, he thought he would maximize his suitor's pleasure by unreeling the much more narrow forked tongue in his mouth, tantalize Sary's anus, and thus afford a more complete ornamental stimulus which he hoped would be of a kind unrealizable to the present experience of women of the earth.

He would be quite correct, as well, as he engaged himself thus, in a manner of metaphor, as an organic "apparatus" whose singular purpose was to entreat as thoroughly as possible the full range of a woman's sexual response.

Thet's a-workin', thet's a-workin'...

Sary's orgasms, though not as lengthy as those manufactured by his sperm, did indeed suffice to leave her quaking, shrieking, and spasming with previously unknown pleasures. When her nerves had fully liquidated their capacity to orgasm, Wilbur recalled all appendages, while Sary lay in a near comatose state, so potent were the rigors of her delight.

Thar's the ticket, ee-yuh. She look more happy'n a egg-suck dog in a blammed hen house, he thought. It was a quip his grandfather used to say.

Wilbur could not have been more regaled. He relit the lamp, then briefly left her inert while he washed, dried himself, and donned clean clothes. His own penis, energized by the visual excitement of Sary's nudity, had now assumed a semi-turgid state as his body struggled to beget more of his alchemical spermatozoa. He felt a great assurance that by morning he would have undergone more than enough refraction, whereupon more proper intercourse would ensue. His grandfather had once said, *Willy, when a fella's wore his pecker out on a gull, he needs ta take TIME afore his dick got more goods ta give up.* Therefore, Wilbur took this simple pearl of wisdom to heart. There would surely be more "goods" available after a sufficient passage of time.

He gathered up his canvas carry-sack, filled with the few things he might need (a small crow bar, for instance, and his pistol). A moment was all that he needed to take pen in hand and scribble a quick note, which he left conspicuously on the desk top.

Gawd, I love her, he mused, his eyes agaze at Sary's sleeping form. He retraced his steps back to the cot, to plant a fragile kiss on her lips.

Then he left the tool-house, quietly closed the door behind him, and ventured out into the vast and illimitable night.

SIXTEEN

It was three gentle chimes to which Sary found herself waking, with a mist of lamplight filling the room. A second's confusion, then the memory of her previous seizure of pleasure resurfaced, which sired a delighted moan. But a quick sweep of her hand made it clear: Wilbur was not in bed with her.

Whar could he be at THIS hour?

A tickling sensitivity flared within her sex when she rose nude from the cot. Had Wilbur gone out to check the traps? Or perhaps he was tending to the smoker. But the sliver of yellow light from the oil lamp seemed to impart a summons, so she drifted to it...

She turned up the wick, to discover a sheet of paper awaiting her on the immense desk. It read:

Deer Sary: Only the hevens know how I about have a fit just bein away from you for even a minnute. But I didnt want to wake you, figuring how tired you likely be. I hadd to go to the generul store in Aylesbury ta fetch me somethin them cads at Osborn's don't got. It be a long walk, I know, but do not wurry yourself becuaze you can rest sure that I'll be back by time the sun rise, and will likewise be thinkin about you til then.

Adoringly,
Wilbur

Sary felt a prickly heat of gratuity by the thoughtful last line, as well as the "Adoringly"; but reason did not take long to occur to her. *Why he goin' to Aylesbury NAOW? Their general store en't open, and nor is any other at this hour...* As had happened so many times thus far, Sary found that her exhaustion had been surmounted by inquisitiveness. And she didn't like the idea of Wilbur being about so late. He'd implied that many in Dunwich kept him in ill-regard, so the same might be true of Aylseburians. Her svelte shadow crossed the floor as she meandered about the room; then she found herself standing before the carved bureau wherein Wilbur had examined something earlier in the day. As she recalled, it had been in the top drawer.

I know I shouldn't, but...

She opened the top drawer.

Beside the decomposed books with no bindings there sat a square tin whose top read Mavis Talcum Powder. She pulled off the top.

Bullets...

Pistol bullets, by the looks of them. One of them she picked up and was barely able to read the numbers *.455* along the rim at the bottom of the cartridge. The bullet was crusty with tarnish, even pitted, and stained darkly from age; an examination of the remaining projectiles revealed an identical state. Had these been the things she'd heard *clinking!* when Wilbur had consulted the drawer?

Sary shook her head, vexed. What her lover felt inclined to "fetch" at this hour she could not estimate. The image that kept intruding upon her curiosity, though, was the constant reminder as to *just how good* the sex had been before he'd left. *What did he DO?* she wondered. He'd seemed pain-staken to keep the light out; Sary hadn't been able to see a thing. How could the man have possibly administered to her in so many places and so many ways? And all at the *same time?*

When she focused on the quality of the orgasm—

Ooooo!

—her vagina lurched once very hard, in a shadow-climax itself. The involuntary spasm only reminded her just how much she adored Wilbur's love-making; and how desperately she wished to have more of the same.

She turned with some force, to divert herself from such libidinous thoughts. Now she stood before the big desk and all its fascinating clutter. What Wilbur had most recently been writing revealed itself to be more of the uncipherable script she'd already seen. She allowed her eyes to scan the letter slots, then the neat little drawers, but, as if driven by some unknown revenant, she was next focused on the large, hoary book with iron hinges.

It lay open, and she read a passage:

Curs'd be ye Ground wherein Dead Musings doth live Revigor'd and Oddly Bodied, and Evill is ye Brain which be supporteth by no Head.

Sary stared at the words. When she'd looked at the book that first day, she'd detected desultory nauseousness, but now...
She felt...*interesting.*
She flipped a page, and read another passage:

Negotium perambulans in tenebris. . . .

Sary flinched at the ghost of a sensation: very nearly that of an urgent hand cupping her crotch, then squeezing her there.
Another page:

Ye Affair which shambleth about in ye night, ye Evil which defieth ye Elder Sign, ye Herd which stand watch at ye guard'd by-waye each tomb be known to possess, and which feedeth on that which groweth out of ye tenants therein—

Upon finishing the bizarre passage (which she understood *nothing* of) Sary was surprised to find the furrow of her sex slick with lubrication; moreover, her nipples stood out, having given over to a delicious buzz. Her immediate impulse was to pinch said nipples to goad more sensation; and to stimulate her sex with her hand. Her eyes, however, seemed to move out of tandem with her brain.
A further passage:

Yog-Sothoth be ye key to ye gate.

A hot gust caught in Sary's chest. She stepped away from the book as if overwhelmed; and though her mind was blank, she could feel her right hand burrowing into her sex to the wrist. Bewildered, she drew it out, and stared at the book. *It's some kind'a magic...,* she presumed, even knowing that she had little belief in such things. Her sex continued to twitch in the weird pre-climatic pulses.

The book was having a tangible effect on her. Sary decided to flip to yet another page, and see what happened...

Upon ye absence of ye ashe of Ibn Ghazi, a heartfull myrmidon shalt do good, in ordereth to take into thine eyes that whicheth maye naught be seen, thou must needs partake in ye deft pracktice of ye sign know'd most Especiall as ye Voorish Sign, which maye be done as thus:

And here the transcription came to a surcease, to depict instead a series of similar sketches whose quality of illustration seemed the work of no unskilled artist. There were five sketches all told; the first was a sketch of a human hand (a left hand) with its ring- and middle-fingers curled downward; and the thumb touching the pinky. The four sketches remaining each featured the same undetailed male figure, showing this sequence:

The figure brought its awkwardly configured hand to its mouth.

Then the hand touched the left pectoral.

Then the abdomen.

Then the forehead.

At once Sary recalled Wilbur making this same gesture the other day! Initially she'd been reminded of a priest making the sign of the Cross, but then saw the nullifying incongruities.

She could perceive no harm. She stilled herself where she stood, then, consulting the diagram for guidance, manipulated her hand as designated, and then—

145

Heer goes...
—made the antediluvian Voorish Sign.
Wal?
Sary's shoulders drooped several moments after she'd completed the gesture. Nothing untoward became obvious to her; the room remained unchanged. But then again—
What effect did she expect to be made privy to?
A more practical way to spend her time was what occurred to her next; hence, she turned—
—gaped—
—and froze as if caught in the glare of the Medusa.
The lamplight well revealed a very peculiar presence on the cot: the presence of a *woman* (and one apparently impinged upon by a number of congenital defects), lying naked, heaving, glazed in sweat, and spread-legged upon the hand-made mattress. What's more, the trespasser's harrowing *uncomeliness* came as a shock equal to that of the inexplicable fact of her being here. First noticed was her skin, an unhealthy pinkish white, with the faintest blue veins coursing beneath. Next, her hair: ash-white, in an unkempt eruption of kinkiness, both upon her head and betwixt her legs. Four toes were evident on one foot, six on the other; and one arm was clearly longer than its counterpart. Weirder were the woman's eyes, which alternately opened and closed from the sensory result of what she was doing: her irises were pink, while the whites shone a pale, sickish yellow. And weirder even than *that?* The right breast jutted plumply, but the left sagged to the mattress like a two-foot-long skin-sock. The nipples of both more resembled plops of chewed jerky. Had Sary been less distracted by the sheer alarm of her discovery, she might also have noticed suspicious configurations of *scar tissue*—as of scars from repeated *incisions*—congregated about the intruder's throat and areolae.
But these oddities, along with the oddity of the woman's presence in the tool-house, were utterly superseded by the activity she now very fervently partook of. She was masturbating with a teardrop-shaped summer squash more than twelve inches in length. The woman engaged in this process in the manner of a ramrod, inserting the squash's

widest end first, and then dragging it quickly and arduously back and forth. Clearly, her vagina was well-acclimated to the admission of objects of such size. Each thrust forward caused the woman's buttocks to clench and her malformed feet to curl; and each extraction—so wide was the squash—threatened to exteriorize her vaginal barrel. An acorn-sized clitoris protruded with each repetition.

Beside her, arranged in a row, lay more objects which she evidently planned to insert into herself: a pickax handle, a wine bottle, a very fat dead snake.

Eventually the squash's physical integrity succumbed to the burden that had been wrought upon it; and collapsed to wedges within the woman's sex. She hastily withdrew the pieces, then reached for the pickax handle...

That was all. The woman disintegrated, just as campfire smoke would vanish at a modest breeze.

What the HAIL I jess see? Sary interrogated herself.

A ghost?

Was she seeing things?

Was she sick?

But the outrageous woman had been as plain—and as real—as day. A dash to the cot, and the placement of Sary's hand upon the mattress, supported this contention: there was a minor aggregation of dampness there, and heat, as if someone had quitted the mattress only seconds ago. Then...

Wait a minute...

She'd seen the woman immediately after she'd made that hand-motion from the old book.

The Voorish Sign...

Sary configured the fingers of her left hand, took a breath, and made the sign once more, while looking with great intent at the cot.

The anemic woman did not make a reappearance.

Sary went back to the tome, looked up at an inclination, then shouted, "Holy *BULL-flop!*"

It was now an ancient man who stood before her. Grayish-black crinkly hair bloomed about his head, and he had a beard identical to the hair; it was much like Wilbur's hair and beard, along with the recessive chin. But this oldster was short, bow-backed, spindly, dressed not in the laboring-attire of the day but in black trousers, black shoes and tunic—like an outre priest. About his neck hung a flat metal pendant, depicting what Sary could only guess was a malformed head with snakes trailing from it. Spectacular gems surrounded the monstrous effigy, stones like rubies but striated with threads of obsidian-black. Also of note were several lines of scar tissue on his throat, incisions made long ago.

The man looked at Sary crazy-eyed, though there was an undisputable shade of *approval* in his overall cast. His lips moved emphatically yet gave no voice. He was nodding.

Then he, too, disintegrated.

WHAT is goin' ON?

This question, a qualified one, would regrettably be commuted to uselessness in only a moment.

Before Sary could long cogitate the meaning of what she'd just witnessed, she flinched, and her heart skipped, as—

CRUNCH!

—the sudden sound assaulted her ears. Did it remind her of wood planks being pried away?

A murmur akin to voices followed the noise.

Sary rushed to the small window.

Outside, in moonlight more than profuse, a male figure busied himself before the saturnine house, in his hand a crowbar. *Aw, noooooooo,* Sary thought, for she recognized the trespasser: Joe Czanek, a local idler whose repute was that of a poacher and petty thief. Last year, the man had paid Sary a dime for sex; whereupon he'd kicked her hard as he might between the legs, choked her unconscious, copulated with her to satisfaction, revived her by urinating in her face, took his money back, and tromped off, laughing. The reason for the man's presence here was obvious enough: he was crow-barring the planks off one of the downstairs windows of Wilbur's house, sporting burglary as his motive.

This, however, was not Sary's most salient concern.

Of late, Joe Czanek was seldom seen out of the company of his partner, a drifter and former state incarceree named

Manny Silva. Mr. Silva had raped Sary on several occasions, and not without the accompaniment of some diverse violence and appalling degradation. What much troubled Sary was this: *I see Joe Czanek right thar, so where might Manny Silva be?*

BAM!

The shed door broke open, by the impact of a large, booted foot belonging to the subject of her last question. "I *knowed* I heerd me suthin' inside this li'l shit-house. And look who it be!" Manny Silva guffawed. "Stew Face, weerin' nary a stitch!"

He was fat, had a lazy left eye and a curious hole in his right cheek. Seeing Sary so abruptly nude transformed his plump face into a portraiture of lust-soused diablerie. Before Sary could move to defend herself, the abdominous home-invader (drooling through the cheek-hole) deployed himself in a tactic which cornered Sary, and then—

THUNK!

Silva had lunged, slamming the prostitute against the wall, an act which deprived her of all energy and air. "Yes, sar! Jess wait'll Joe git a gander'a *yew!*" he speculated, then grabbed his victim by her tuft of pubic hair and conveyed her from the tool-house out into the sultry night. Sary's head and shoulder-blades scuffed along the ground, around the shed, and out to the front of Wilbur's boarded-up house.

"Hey, Joe! Take a look-see!"

On her back, Sary wheezed breath, blinking spots out of her vision. By the time she was vaguely sensate, two moonlight-forged silhouettes stood over her, arms crossed in valuation. She heard black chuckles, and then—

Kurrrrrrr-HOCK

—one of them spat on her.

"Wal what have we heer?" Czanek, the thinner criminal, posed. "Never thunk *any* gull would have the stomach ta take up with Wilbur Whateley."

"I heerd he en't got *no balls!*"

"Probably no dick, neither!"

Dizzy, Sary croaked her proverbial two-cents' worth. "Wilbur be *double* the man'a both a yew combined."

"Yeah?"

"And I heerd yew fellas suck each other, then swap the cum," Sary added.

The men laughed. "Do we naow?"

Belts came unfastened, trousers were lowered. Right now, Sary needed no capacity for interpreting matters beyond the range of ordinary perception; she was not surprised, in other words, when both miscreants began to urinate on her. Why destiny had seen to insist that Sary be pissed on *so many times in her life* was a puzzle she suspected had no solution. But she knew well that far worse was in store for her tonight.

"Now *thar's* haow it's done," Czanek's black words blared. "En't nuthin' more finer'n pissin' on a gull a'fore ya fuck her."

"Yes, sar!" cracked Silva (whose urine, for whatever arcane reason, tasted *spicy*). "My pa tolt me the same thing yeers ago!"

"Weren't my pa who told me," Czanek recollected. "'Twas my *ma.* 'Tis a good rasher'a kidney juice what make a woman know her place."

Both men maintained their urine streams for a full minute without so much as a decline; to Sary, however, it felt more like an hour. When she summoned some strength, and made to lunge away—

THWUP!

—one of the interlopers stomped on her belly.

Sary again was pilfered of all her wind. She could do nothing but gasp and cringe as her two visitors *continued* to urinate with a copiousness which seemed more equine than human. But when they at last had no more "kidney juice" at their disposal, Sary remained sufficiently paralyzed from the abdominal blow. What she heard, with the hard moonlight in her eyes, were sounds akin to those of men undressing in anticipatory haste. Then?

A *causerie,* since the debauched chat which followed could not be dignified by the word "conversation."

"Dang, talk about some dandy luck. Fust we see Wilbur headin' daown the rud toward Aylesbury"—he pronounced the word "toward" as *terd*—"and then we find this 'un buck naked in his shed."

"And with Wilbur goin' all the way aout thar, it en't likely he'll be back a'fore marnin'."

"Plenny a time ta search that big ole pile'a shit haouse of his, and find all the gold he got hid in thar."

"Yes, sar! An' plenny'a time ta fuck this *hoo-uh* raw!"

A chuckle. "Wonder what ole Wilbur'll think when he come home'n find his tramp full'a *our cum!*"

This was the manner of colloquy that Sary's dizzied attention rewarded her with. So it was the gold they hoped to find within the house? Sary knew it was not there, but instead somewhere in the woods, for that's from whence Wilbur had trekked when he'd given her the coin...

She began the grim speculation in her mind, *When they dun't find it in the haouse...,* but there was no advantage in finishing, for it would be granted that the likes of these two would torture her with an unprecedented vigor in order to be apprized of where the gold might be.

The truth made her feel gypped, as it often did in her life. *Wilbur wun't be back fer quite a spell, and likely as not, I'll be dead when he git heer.* Rogues such as Czanek and Silva would hardly leave a living witness to their crimes.

If only she could somehow slip away long enough to regain the tool-house, secure a knife or other weapon, and at least die fighting.

"I fucked this one a'fore," Czanek remarked. His shadow appeared to be *flapping* its penis.

"Aw, yeah. Me, too, bunch'a times. Didn't piss on her, mind ya, but I shore as hail *shit* on her, and rubbed her face in it tew. Then I gave her a boot shampoo as to go with it."

"Watch this," Czanek suggested. "See, what *I* always do 'fore a fuck a gull, see, I give her a good hard kick in the cunt."

"Yew dew?"

Czanek's gaunt silhouette nodded. "Reason ta dew that is on accaount when ya cunt-kick her hard enough? It make her pussy swell all up inside, and get'cha a tighter hole up in 'nar for ya to get your dick in."

151

Silva's silhouette stared still as if the entirety of Immanuel Kant's doctrine on Transcendental Idealism had just been imparted to him with full comprehension. "Why...I never thunk'a that."

"Aw, yeah. *Always* cunt-kick a gull 'fore ya fuck her. 'Tis a waste not tew," and with this, Cnazek walked around to Sary's feet, bent over, grabbed her heels, pushed her legs far back, and—

"Gander this, Manny. I'se gonna cunt-kick her *so hard,* her baby-maker'll come up her maouth!"

Sary still could scarcely move. The prospect of Wilbur arriving for a rescue as timely as he had at Osborn's seemed to present a very low order of probability. Instead, she resigned to this atrocity, remembering well her short time with Wilbur and how happy he'd made her. She turned her head aside, staring barrenly. Waiting...

What she saw, though—and with an unbidden yet insistent focus—was the very window that had been previously vandalized by the talents of Monsieur Czanek. All the boards had been pried away, and the frame itself too. This left a gaping black oblong hole...

"Git reddy!" Silva exclaimed as Czanek poised his kicking leg.

"Git set!"

Czanek pulled his leg back farther.

"Aaaaaaaaaaaand..."

Sary remained too dizzy even to pray, but her bedimmed mind managed a final gesture: *Yew take keer, Wilbur Whateley. Hope ya know I love yew...*

The extra second which Silva would require to yell "Go!" would not be provided, nor would Czanek have opportunity to propel his foot forward against the desired abutment of Sary's sexual aperture. Instead, both men seemed to seize in place, their heads cocking toward a faint, even barely audible sound.

Was it a *hissing?* Or more semblant to a *slithering,* as of a snake advancing rapidly?

Sary's eyes remained peeled on the vicinity of the agape

window. Just below this stretched a portion of scrub grass, which—

Sary squinted in the moonlight.

The grass was *moving*. As if, indeed, a snake were traversing there.

But in this case, it would have to be an *invisible* snake.

Joe Czanek and Manny Silva, with a suddenness as if catapulted, left their place on the ground and *flew up into the air*. They roved there, not as if flung but as if via some manner of controlled suspension—that is...an *invisible* controlled suspension. Screams took little time to issue from both of the airborne gentlemen, screams which might mirror an abstraction as those of human souls held helpless and *ad perpetuum* in the clutches of perdition.

In truth, these two valueless sociopaths were in the clutches of something else altogether.

Into Sary was injected an amount of adrenalin more than commensurate to efface her pain and bleared consciousness, and to locomote her with an excess of speed to the edge of the tool-house. Circumstance left her no option but to stare into the moonlit area before the house and behold the unbelievable sight. Her two accosters continued to belt out blood-spraying screams as they continued, too, to rove about in the mid-air. By moonlight, Sary could see well that they were fully naked, and could see *too* well every depressing detail of their fish-belly-white bodies, their horror-diminished genitals, and the splats of excrement blurting from their bowels. Each scream stepped up as their uncanny hovering went on. Were bones heard cracking? And was some inexplicable distortion suddenly effecting the abdominal regions of both men? Sary felt certain that Joe Czanek's waist *collapsed* for no discernible reason; again, the "snake" parallel came to mind, for many times on her walks she'd witnessed snakes subduing squirrels, rats, and such by constricting about the mammals' bodies. When the snakes unreeled to reposition themselves, their prey displayed mid-sections that were collapsed in a corkscrew fashion...

Manny Silva's more corpulent physique distorted to a degree that might even be called spectacular; suddenly he was a sack of suet bisected by a tightening string. Whatever was happening here alarmed Sary so much as to becloud her cognizance entirely. Therefore she wasn't really even aware of what she did next...

She made the Voorish Sign.

If her jaw could've actually come detached and dropped off, it likely would have. Sary could now see the invisible "snakes" which had wrapped about the thieves and held them aloft.

But these snakes were an incarnadine color, a foot-wide, dozens of yards long, and overlain with what seemed to be countless cup-shaped outdents, which, had Sary any ken with aquatic zoology, she might have likened to the tentacular suckers of octopi and other similar cephalopoda.

The tentacles seemed to revel in what their capture yielded; they reeled back and forth displaying the duet of prizes—indeed, almost as if to display them *to Sary herself.* More than feces rained down now, but blood too, exiting mouth and anus alike due to the constricitve pressure. Were Czanek's *lungs* actually dangling from his lips? And what wagged wetly beneath Silva's fat legs was a *tail* of intestines. But more curious than any of this was the *point of origin* of these monstrous appendages:

The vandalized window.

At this point, the tentacles began to withdraw back into the ragged portal, taking their human rewards with them. But before they'd retracted fully into the house, they disintegrated to nothingness, just as had the old man and the insatiable albino woman.

Sary knew very little just then, but she knew *this:* however perilous the prospect might be, she would have to see *all* of what was in Wilbur's house. She would have to behold with her own eyes what manner of *thing* existed at the other end of those "snakes."

She very slowly rose to her feet, and in an automatonic state returned to the tool-house, took up the lantern, and walked back through the moonlight to the house—

To the *window.*

She maximized the lantern's wick and was at once cocooned by licks of wavering yellow light. She thrust the lantern into the aperture, then set it back down after seeing nothing whatever inside. The phrasal idiom *No time like the present* was not one with which Sary had any conversance, but her own unenlightened grey matter managed something correspondent. She stared into the window's Acherontic blackness as she prepared again to make the sign. Something, though, gave her pause.

A feeling. A *notion* whose origin could not be terrestrially identified. Sary sensed—as people were wont to do—the distinct and singular impression of being watched—no, more— of being *gazed upon* with intentness, even deliberateness; but this was stemmed in far more than the commonplace and rather prosaic fear of the unknown. An altogether different persuasion of fear infected Sary as the house interior (and its nearly corporeal darkness) commandeered her gaze. Was it really fear? It seemed so, for her heart raced, she trembled acutely, her molars were chattering, yet these denominators of the emotion in question ended resolutely, and were then accompanied by traits clearly *unrepresentative* of the same.

The lubriciousness within her sex—in a single mental *throb*—grew so teeming that such sequent fluids ran openly down the inside of her thighs; and with each contraction of her heart there came an equal contraction of her *genitals*—ghosts of orgasms that seemed part of her natural state at the present time. It was the darkness past the ravaged window, she knew (something not as much a darkness as a *reckoning, audient physicalization*) and some constituent therein proving to be far more than a simple retardation of light. She could sense it thick in the air, while the air—inscrutable as it might sound— seemed surcharged with not only awareness but also some catalytic *attribute* that seeped into her blood. It *histrionicized* her nudity; it fired conduction in nerves hitherto unsparked; it ignited *mycoplasmic triggers* to permit of sensation thus far unrealized and unfelt; it tickled the very *gene-markers* hidden deep amongst the neurosecretory *pieces of minims* that comprised every fiber of every living cell. Sary's breasts hummed in reactivity; her ovaries vibrated like hummingbirds caught in one's hand; while hormones transmogrified into *new* hormones, and gusted forth from her pituitary gland to drench her libidinal receptors; and the orgasmic spasms of her genitals migrated directly—like an electric bolt—to her brain.

All this, merely by looking into the darkness within the house.

Out of mind now, Sary made the Voorish Sign, thrust the lantern back into the window, and looked—

Was it some imp of the perverse that decoded the retinal images in Sary's eyes and directed them into her memory? Her first glimpse into the bizarre house brought with it a paradoxical unconsciousness: paradoxical in that she seemed to behold herself and her surroundings as if drifting above her physical body; hence, a consciousness within *un*consciousness. Had her very spirit evacuated her body, to move about and to *see?* If so, in what manner of vessel did her spirit now abode?

This question, and a superfluity of others, would occur to her in rapid succession only to be just as rapidly discarded as inconsequential. Matters of far greater signification were at hand...

Her nude body lay dormant beneath her, and Sary noted the clarity in which she saw it, as if through some slightly distorted yet harrowingly accurate lens which revealed every pore of her skin, every razor-sharp black hair upon her head and betwixt her legs, each individual lacteal duct of her areolae, etc. She then raised her head (in a manner of speaking, of course, since whatever now served as quarterage for her sensibilities no longer enjoyed a physical connexion to her body) in order to pilot her sense of sight into the confines of the house. The two tentacles she'd previously glimpsed absconding with the ruffians were now joined by *dozens* more, each tipped by mouths which snapped open and shut in some celebrative synchrony. Those first two tentacles, however, still reeled about, grasping the now quite dead Manny Silva and Joe Czanek; and had Sary a greater capacity for linear thinking, she would've wondered what the appendages had in store for the two miscreant corpses. Instead, all of her attention fixed on the morphological madness and physical contradiction that existed within. Did the scores of stovepipe-thick tentacles change from blue to grey to purple as they also swelled and shrank as if to a premeditated rhythm? Ultimately, the living bulk looked like it had outgrown its shelter to such a degree that very little further growth would be permitted before the house erupted; indeed, so close were the massive thing's boundaries that Sary could scarcely see deep enough through the tentacles to espy what manner of *body* existed to sport the appendages. Might it be akin to the torso of a mammal? The carapace of a crustacean? Or the plasmic sheath of a bacillus cell? Inexplicable, too, was the manner in which the thing seemed to *phase in and out* of various states of being. First came a state of palpable *organum;* then a less composited state, as of jelly or mucus; then a state of distinct semi-solidness, akin to compressed vapor.

Was this incalculable creature's physical mass edging into and out of a dimensional realm contrary to that of the known *three* dimensions?

If Sary were to learn this question's answer, it would not be today.

When she looked again, the corpse of Czanek was being dragged slowly in and out of the mouth-end of a broader tentacle, and each withdrawal dissolved or in some way abraded the cadaver's flesh. (One might've thought of a child sucking a popsicle.) Eventually little remained save for bones, whereupon these, too, were admitted into the tentacular mandibles and swallowed whole. But Sary had been mistaken about the other corpse—Silva, the fat one—which still twitched with piteous life. From the writhing, impossible congeries, a more petite appendage emerged; it wrapped itself about Silva's genitals—just where the scrotum adjoins the crotch—and slowly tore the organ out at the root. This was swallowed, while more such tentacles converged and consumed Silva's physical form one bite at a time. Lastly, the remnants, like Czanek's, were swallowed and digested.

At this point, something changed.

Sary's unembodied senses felt a decline of temperature and an elevation in proximal air pressure. The incognizable behemoth stilled itself, and Sary interpreted the stasis as an indication of *attention* on the thing's part. Why she would make this interpretation, there was no telling. Nevertheless, she was correct.

The thing, indeed, was *assessing* her.

Then a great many of the appendages which composed its physical form retracted...

Now Sary could see what existed as a foundation for the tentacles, the heart of the artichoke, so to speak. It was a mass of eyes, all which looked upon her in fascination and even respect. A mass of eyes, yes, the height and breadth of the largest pine tree on the property. Each eye seemed to be set in nothing at all akin to a socket but instead some gelatinous substance, and...did this substance also have mouths, or things *like* mouths, situated throughout? It would be pallid to say that this being—entity, creature, what have you—existed with virtually no alliance to the laws of nature as we know them; and it would be just as insufficient to say it was not of this earth. It was far more—and far less—than any of that.

The thing's body seemed to percolate, it seemed to *bubble* within. Its eyes did not blink, for they had no lids with which to do so, but they did variegate in shape, while their irises went from one astral hue to the next—colors, tints, and shades never before beheld by the natives of this planet.

Horrific? Yes. But fascinating as well.

And next?

The great bubbling mass began to *turn.*

Of course, it did not turn as, say, a human being would, nor did it change its position by means of swivelling, or traversing. Instead, the excrescence of its base squirmed and rippled, licensing movement, and said movement could only be voluntary.

It meant to show her something.

When the squirming ceased, the creature had presented to Sary the side of itself that had been previously eclipsed by the lantern-shadows. It was this moment of unalloyed shock and tenebrific revelation that blacked out Sary's gossamer senses and sent her spirit soaring back into her prostrate body. A pair of appendages protracted from the hulk—the same pair, in fact, which had so effectively ended the careers of Messrs. Czanek and Silva—and gently lifted an unconscious Sary from her place just outside the window, then—extending farther—placed her back on the cot in the tool-house. They hovered momentarily, as if contemplating her in some commendable way, then retraced themselves back to the material gibbosity of which they were a part.

The actual sight which so forcefully shot Sary back into stygian realms of unconsciousness was nothing more than this:

The creature's face.

It was a half-face, really, the right side consisting of runnels, bumps, and indescribable contours whose purpose could not be estimated. The left side, however, demonstrated great patchworks of what might actually be *hair,* kinky, black accumulations like sporadic moss; one eye not in keeping at all with the myriad eyes that enshrouded the thing's thorax, complete with lashes and an irregular *brow;* a sagging, lipped orifice that the anti-nature of the thing meant for a mouth; a distinctly recessive chin; and patches of some pale, yellowish covering which hideously resembled *human epidermis.* More clumps of crinkly hair sprouted about the mouth and the side of its face—a cheek?—and there was even a macabre convolution of flesh which bore a suspicious likeness to an *ear.*

Overall, however, this "face"—or the atrocious assemblage of impossibility that sufficed for one—bore a suspicious likeness to *Wilbur's* face.

SEVENTEEN

At a time nearly identical to that during which the criminal denizen Joe Czanek had been breaking into Wilbur's house, Wilbur himself was breaking into a mercantile emporium known as Leffert's Feedstock & General Goods, located in the township of Aylesbury. The mechanical nature of the intrusion had been so easy as to unwarrant exposition; and so were the descriptive details of the interior shop. Wilbur lowered his trousers enough to just expose the two ancillary eyes situated in his hips, and with these he suffered no effort in navigating himself through the shop's utter darkness. A cash-box sat opened beneath the counter, revealing obvious loose bills and change, but the giant occult scholar had not come here with any intention of stealing; his moral posture, in fact, made distasteful—and moreover *unthinkable*—the idea of stealing from someone who hadn't stolen from him. On the contrary, his intention was to leave more than sufficient payment on the counter when he found what it was he needed.

And what he needed was ammunition.

Taking chances—or, worse, taking blessings for granted— was a sin he could not well afford, for tomorrow night, indeed, was the time. He remembered too well the guard dog near the Miskatonic library, and in spite of several physiological advantages, Wilbur knew that the dog was fortified with reflexes which surpassed his own, and harbored fangs and jaws that might very well make simpleton's work of his tentaclettes and even his probosciduct. Wilbur, in fact, had been *plagued* by vicious dogs all his life; he could scarcely embark on a leisurely stroll without some such hostile cur, enraged by his scent, tearing after him. Grandsire's big pistol had forestalled many a canine confrontation, much to the displeasure of the dogs' masters.

But not only was Wilbur running out of bullets for the formidable Webley .455, the cartridges his did possess were so old as to be of questionable reliability. Twice now, he'd had to repel attacks only to have the weapon's hammer fall on a defective primer; and though engaging the next round was but a matter of seconds, seconds were insufficient in certain instances. Wilbur was not afraid to die, but he knew that he must *not* die—or be grievously injured—before he discharged his all-important task on the night of the morrow.

Osborn's had stopped carrying the peculiar caliber Wilbur needed; and even when they'd most recently had it in stock, they'd refused to sell to him. "Ya big ass-ugly freak! Yer face looks like the devil's bunghole, and ye smell even *wuss!*" Tobias railed at him once. "Ye think I'm a-gonna sell ammunition to the likes of *ye?* Ya done already kilt half the dogs in the village, ya cockeyed monster! I'll have me no truck with the blood'a Wizard Whateley! Naow git aout!" Wilbur was surprised not at all by his cousin's hostile rant. "Yer bleach-faced ma sucked my dick onct, fer a haff-pint'a hooch," the old misanthrope saw fit to add. "I pushed up that trash-cloth dress'a hers and gandered her pussy and—sweet Jesus!—the sight give me *nightmares,* boy! Look like a blammed *woodchuck* with a *ax-cut* in it!" Wilbur was none too pleased to hear such talk about his mother, yet he doubted the rant was invention; hence, it wouldn't have been ethical to hex the old man for mere words.

All that aside, the young colossan could ponder no other resort but to travel hither to Aylesbury to procure the necessary bullets. The piddling lock on the ammunition cabinet came apart with a single tug, then—

Disappointment.

The .455 cartridges Wilbur so desperately needed were not in the store's inventory. And since the establishment sold only ammunition, and not firearms as well, Wilbur's trek had been a profitless one.

The gods be a-testin' me, he could only presume, for to exhibit agitation would be to reveal an absence of faith. No time remained for him to venture to another town. *I'll jess have to hope ta Yog-Sothoth that them old bullets I got'll fire.*

Wilbur felt no fear at the prospect. He would simply discharge his task to the best of his ability, or die in the endeavor. Yes, he felt certain beyond doubt: the gods were testing him.

But when the drone came into his head only moments later, he knew that another test was upon him. He'd only just quitted the store and commenced through the woods toward the Aylesbury Pike when he'd stopped to stand stock-still. It wasn't a seizure, nor any manner of ringing in the ears. Instead, this could be described as a *visual* drone, and he knew at once from whence it came.

His brother.

Wilbur, awkwardly as he appeared, ran all the way back home. It was the psychic coupling that existed between himself and his twin brother that had heralded his haste, and that same ethereal tether that showed him most of everything which had occurred back at his grandfather's house, to a level of detail as accurate as if he'd been physically present. Wilbur's clumsy trot foreshortened the several-hour walk to a span of under an hour; and when he arrived at the property—winded, flushed, and oozing netherworldly perspiration—he audibly cried out thanks to his Yog-Sothoth and his retinue when he found Sary asleep and unharmed in the cot. He leaned over, teary-eyed, and kissed her on the cheek. He prepared to depute with exigency to the house but found several trace scents afflicting his nostrils. A dank *reptilian* smell? And the tinge of unwashed female genitals of a particular nature as to remind him of his *mother?* Also a scent apart from all of that, much more concise: cologne. Dunwichers were not known to have much use for cologne but Wilbur could not forget the homemade fragrance his grandfather concocted—with orange-flower oil and lavender—to wear on special occasions. A slow swerve of his head showed him the *Necronomicon* where he'd left it on the desk, no longer opened to Page 751. The ancient sheets of vellum now displayed Page 415, and the transition detailing the proper execution of the Voorish Sign.

That would certainly explain the haunting redolences within the shed.

Outside, the issuance of a chuckle could not be forborne when he discerned no physical vestige of Joe Czanek and Manny Silva. Wilbur envisioned with revel their gruesome deaths, relayed by the connexion betwixt himself and his leviathanic brother, and seen through the latter's plethora of eyes; and he could smell their remains being digested therein. It was a rich, syrupy aroma, as often was the case of vile men who'd died inundated in fear and horror. So acute was that psychic cordage that *Wilbur himself* could faintly taste the reprobate scoundrels like after-flavors upon his own tongue.

At the violated window, he made the Voorish Sign and engaged in some telepathic confabulation. His brother smiled at him—a dolorous smile, of course—and Wilbur nodded and smiled as well. The grim acknowledgment flickered between them, though said acknowledgment came as neither much of a surprise nor much of a shock to either of them.

He boarded the window back up, then turned, cheeks still damp with tears, and he gazed at the lopsided moon. The icy light enlivened him. A beautiful world it truly was...

He whispered praise and thanks, turning for the shed. His strides were made with confidence and resolve. He knew he would not see his brother again.

Sary stood tense and wide-eyed when Wilbur returned to the tool-house. The carriage clock's chime-like peals were just now expending four o'clock in the morning. Wilbur was well aware of the graveness of the situation, but the sight of Sary arrested all possibility of him speaking of it.

Never before had he seen her so beautiful than in just that pristine wee-hour moment.

Naked she remained, her breasts alert, even inflamed. Her body's contours could not have been more preeminent if they'd been chiseled by a Michelangelo or a Desiderio. The flat bright-white of her belly, the curvaceous legs, the stark black wedge of private hair—all converged to project into Wilbur an alchemy of ardor, attraction, and of *love* more empowered than the passion which launched a thousand ships. Against the flawless skin, the lamplight wavered, suggesting a sudden complexity emerging within the simple woman. Her hair spilled about her lambent shoulders like ink blacker than any shadow cast upon the earth.

Her lips parted to speak but a further cogitation stifled them.

She be it, Wilbur knew.

Her wide eyes scintillated; where often they reflected naivety or confusion they now blazed a *keenness* he'd never noticed in her before, not quite the keenness of cabalistic understanding, nor even of revelation—that would arrive later—but a *thirst...*

A thirst to *learn.*

"Sary," Wilbur whispered. This spectacular vision of her parched his throat.

"Sumpin' happened," she whispered back.

"I know it. And I know ye seen it yourself"—his eyes gestured the opened book—"by larnin' ye haow to do the Voorish."

"I hope yew ain't flustered with me fer meddlin' where I shouldn't have been, but...*naow?* I got the feelin' that it's sumpin I *need* to know."

"It 'tis," Wilbur affirmed. "And theer en't no setch thing as meddlin' when it come to one's mind haow they got a *callin'.* A callin' to be part'a suthin' that be bigger'n all of us set together."

To these words, Sary's eyes went ever the wider.

"Them two fellas who come heer dun't caount fer nothin'," he explained. "Mebbe the gods sent 'em special, so to show you suthin'. The gods work that way sometimes. They make us *earn* our blessin's." Wilbur pointed in the direction of the house. "That One in there, wal...it be my brother."

This disclosure alarmed Sary not in the least; indeed, if anything, it answered some of her inner queries, of which there must be a multitude.

"It be my twin, come aout'a my ma right after me, on the Candlemas, 1915. See, I en't old as ye must've supposed. The way I be, I grow fast, and that One inside? It grow ever faster. Where I went tonight was to fetch some new—"

"Bullets," she said in a drone.

"Ee-yuh. On accaount them ones I got in the tin be real old setch that some of 'em dun't fire. But that place didn't have none."

Sary's posture fidgeted.

"Dun't worry. I en't afeared. Either Yog-Sothoth'll protect me, or he wun't, and if he wun't, it only mean I en't worthy."

"We'll know soon," came Sary's cryptic remark.

This was a good sign. She was learning already, simply through the transpositional effect of proximity to Wilbur's brother. It was esoteria. It was science disguised as occult mystery—a pheromonal transduction of *knowledge*—for human sensibility did not exist broadly enough to understand. It *never* had. "We will, for sure," he said. "I'll tell ye what I can tonight, and if'n things go as I gotta mind they might, ye'll larn plennie more in time. Tonight be the night I gotta go—"

"To Arkham," she uttered. "To the college."

"That's right. I need to be there after midnight...when the stars are right."

Finally, Sary moved from where she'd been standing still as an erotic chess piece. She came over and hugged Wilbur desperately.

The words gushed against Wilbur's shirt. "I'm afraid, Wilbur."

"En't no reason to be," he assured her, wrapping his great arms about her. The heat from her naked body seeped into him. "En't no setch things as endin's—Grandsire teached me that. An endin' en't nuthin' but a beginnin' to suthin' else more important—least ways, I mean, for thems that prove themselves desarvin' of the favor of the gods. Them gods? They've *always* been good ta me."

She was shivering. "I'm afraid for *yew*. That somethin' bad'll happen."

"En't nuthin' bad *can* happen ta me," he began to assure her, but then thought it more serviceable to leave off the rest of the doctrinal explanation: the City between the magnetic

165

poles, the Dho and the Dho-Hna, the *Spiritum in Aeternum,* the Yr and the Nhhngr, and the Transfiguration. She would learn it all at the proper time, from the book. "Nor nuthin' ta happen ta ye, neither," he whispered. "That I sware afore all I hold dear."

Wilbur leaned back and took off his shirt. Sary did not recoil—she *rejoiced*—at this full sight of his writhing, mouth-tipped tentaclettes. She seemed to turn boneless in his strong arms, her sex running with excited fluids. His probosciduct reared, then gently entered her vagina, to pulsate; while a salvo of tentaclettes converged upon her nipples and clitoris, to ever-so-gingerly suck.

Wilbur carried Sary to the cot, lowered her there, then turned out the lantern.

Most of the final twenty-four hours of Wilbur Whateley's life can only be epitomized via estimation, not documentation. It can, though, be authoritatively intimated that the physical demonstrations of his love for Sary were most copious— indeed, such that for her final few hours she would spend in his proximity, she could barely stand on her own two feet. It was true that Wilbur needed to be inconspicuously deployed near the main library of Miskatonic University no later than midnight on August third, when the Moon assumed a nine-degree ecliptic belt, and Antares, Saturn, and Betelgeuse formed a Cavalieri right triangle; this would require Wilbur to part from Sary's company by two p.m. on the second, so that he might engage the bus that would permit of his venture to Arkham. Sary struggled to stand when her lover made this information plain, demanding, "Won't take me a speck of time to get dressed," she asserted, "and I'll come with yew," but Wilbur had no choice but to disallow the offer, in spite of its kindliness. "Naw, Sary, mutch as I'd like ta have ye with me, it jess carn't be. Yew best stay here, but with any luck, I'll be back tomorrow afternoon, sence them's the ways the bus work, for it only run twice a day." "No!" she rejected, "I'm comin' with yew! I've got a mind yew plan ta steal a book they got at the college, and I gotta mind tew it'll be dangerous!"

166

Wilbur was quite taken by the expeditiousness with which she presumed to assist him, yet still he had to say, "I wun't let ye come with me, Sary, for 'tis true, mebbe it 'twill be dangerous, and there en't no way on the airth that I'll allow no harm ta git near ye. And it ain't stealin' I'm fixin' ta do, jess...borrowin'." Fatigued from the previous tumult of intercourse and sexual variation, Sary nearly toppled trying to get into her dress, but she managed a most indignant glare, pointed a finger, and exclaimed, "I'm a-*goin'*, Wilbur Whateley, and if yew think'a leavin' withaout me, I will pitch a fit far wuss than any storm yew ever see!" "I got me no daoubt ye would," Wilbur replied, and smiled deeply at her resolve. What a wonder this was. All his life he never thought the day would dawn when a woman would demand to be part of his life. *Ee-yuh, I love her sooooo mutch. Thank ye, Yog-Sothoth...* "Sorry ye carn't have your way on this, Sary," he began, still smiling his love for her as recited one of the Eltdown Languor Spells which made her fall asleep so fast she did so on her feet. Wilbur caught her, held her a while, and put her to bed. He looked at her with adoration, and whispered, "I love ye, Sary."

Then he grabbed his canvas carry-sack and took his leave of the tool-house.

Sary's perceptivity, however, was quite on the mark. Though Wilbur wasn't *sure* of the evening's outcome, some assistance would prove very advantageous. Out on the Aylesbury Pike, when his awkward form arrived at the bus stop, it was none other than Kyler the psychic who was arriving as well. "Hey, Kyler," Wilbur greeted. "Yew a-waitin' on the bus?" "Aye, jest as are ye," the eccentric black-clad man replied. "Though it may not be credited by ye that I am subject to portents mysterious indeed, I've received it of goodly authority that it may be in ye're best interest to have me near."

Wilbur nodded, amused. "I never said I dun't believe yew're a soothsayer—"

The bright sun shined on the lame man's bald head, though his face remained peculiarly shadowed. "For what ye be in sarch of come in the waye of letters."

Letters, Wilbur thought with a pause. Did the cryptic man with the cane mean letters as of correspondence? Or letters, as of...the alphabet? Wilbur had no choice but to ponder this with some fascination.

"And for they who venture well into the night? Wal, oft times, when one be not on his proper guard," Kyler went on with nonchalance, "the night comes bearing teeth."

Teeth, Wilbur thought. *That dang guard dog...*

After a time, Wilbur said, "I be mutch obliged if ye come with me, Kyler, for I may well need ta ask a favor."

Kyler nodded. "Aye, if I could only ask ye to pay my fare."

"Oh, a'course, I will. 'Tis the least I can dew. As well I can offer ye this gold piece so's ya know the extent'a my gratitude," and then Wilbur offered him a mint-condition Saxon Offa coin struck in 1011 A.D., which would easily bring in ten dollars from a jeweler (but a thousand dollars from a qualified collector or auction house.)

"Nay, Wilbur. No money can be took by me from a friend."

Wilbur consented to the wish, but would secret the coin into Kyler's bag when he was unaware.

Just down the road, then, a dervish-like cloud of dust was rising. It was the bus to Arkham.

EIGHTEEN

This portion of the narrative, as the finish approaches, might be regarded by some as disproportioned, but this can only be blamed on Fate—as the structure of life itself rarely issues in satisfactory equipoise. Wilbur Whateley did indeed encounter the end of his physical life in the early hours of August the third, in the Rare Books cove of Miskatonic Library. He was savaged by the guard dog which prowls the entire building at night, and evidently some appreciable time had lapsed between the gigantic man's unlawful entrance and the point at which the animal detected his presence. There was evidence of a candle being lit, and of Wilbur's effort to *write* something quickly with pen and paper. What this *something* was would remain a fair mystery to the academic trio who discovered Wilbur's body; though one of the three, Dr. Henry Armitage, had the notion that the ungainly intruder had been translating and, hence, transcribing a section of the college's Latin edition of *The Necronomicon,* stanzas that might correspond to Page 751 of the 1582 English edition. However, no transcription was found, so if it existed...what had become of it? Armitage could only make an educated estimation.

After the corpse had disintegrated, one of Armitage's associates, Professor Rice, had pointed to a canvas sack askew on the floor, and made the supposition, "He must have meant to steal *The Necronomicon* and carry it off in that."

"I'd think not, Warren," came the elder's reply, "for surely a man—or thing—as astute as Wilbur Whateley would have calculated in advance the sack's insufficient size. No, I believe he came here to copy something from the Latin, but I can only guess—since no transcription is present—that a partner of some sort made off with it."

"You mean a *second* perpetrator?" asked Dr. Francis Morgan.

Armitage pinched his chin in contemplation. "It seems so to me, gentlemen." Now that much of the stench had cleared, he walked to an ancillary exit door which locked from the inside. "I unlocked the vestibule door myself, but *this* door?"

Rice and Morgan saw at once that the access had been—

"Unlatched," Rice observed.

"So unless the security man was uncharacteristically lax tonight," Morgan continued, "this door here was indeed unlocked from the inside, by Whateley himself."

"Yes," Armitage agreed, "which might give more credulity to my theory of a second party."

Rice was nodding. "After violating the east window here, Whateley let his confident in through this door."

Close examination at a later time revealed that Wilbur had arrived with full knowledge of the guard dog's threat, as a large pistol was found near the central desk, its hammer having clearly fallen on a defective cartridge. So swift the watch dog's reflexes had been, that the awkward giant had insufficient time to forward the cylinder to the next round.

It was as simple as that.

Not so simple was the aspect of the decedent's body. There were few who disbelieved that an intruder had died in the room, for the repute of the three witnesses was not contestable, even as the details of the corpse remain a matter of private record, not public. It was actually better that way, for what might the masses interpret about the *aspect* of such a dead body? Better, too, in the long run, that the *corpus delecti* had actually vanished via some mode of disintegration before a camera could be procured for recording such evidence.

No description of Wilbur's naked body will be conveyed; it will only be said instead that the dog had attacked the colossal man with the savagery expected of it, and ripped off most of the trespasser's attire along with unpleasantly large swatches of his epidermis—if it could be *called* epidermis. Within minutes of the occult scholar's death, no vestige of the man's physical mass remained, save for some morbid whitish liquefaction. This too would disappear completely just as the medical examiner arrived. The man—or entity—had disappeared as if he—or it—had never existed.

In the weeks following, no clue would be imparted to Armitage as to the identity of Wilbur's "associate"; while all ponderment over the question would disappear as effectively as Wilbur had himself, in the second week of September, when the Dunwich Horror (in the form of Wilbur's twin brother) had erupted from its confines and gone on a futile and even pitiable rampage. After *this,* though, once the Whateley property had been certified as safe to examine, Armitage inspected the premise personally after having received, as per his instructions, all written material, letters, diaries, and books left by the departing giant.

Armitage would spend the rest of his life investigating the horrific affair, yet would receive no reward for his effort. This failure would actually haunt the academician, such that he'd often feel he had lost some abstract battle with the dead giant he'd once sent out of his library. The doctor would have wagered his life that Wilbur Whateley had indeed copied Page 751 of the Latin edition and relayed it to someone else. So the question reared with some significance, even to the point of the doctor's own death: who had absconded with these transcriptions?

And why?

After wakening from the Languor Spell, Sary slept not at all for the entire night. Instead, she paced, worried, and looked repeatedly out the shed's door in the dim hope that Wilbur might return early.

But she could not wrest away from the conviction that he would not.

At day-break, having no familiarity with the timetable for the Arkham bus route, she straggled morosely to the crude bus-stop post, and waited.

She waited some time, until past the noon-hour, in fact. Her heart gave an excited thump at sight of the rattletrap vehicle; then she jittered on her feet, hands clasped in prayer, when the smoke-belching motor slowed and stopped. The door flapped open, but the sinking feeling had already afflicted her—either a premonition or an umbra of pessimism—for she'd felt begloomed since she'd last seen Wilbur yesterday, and this feeling had worsened since a nervous nauseousness had struck her past sun-up, such that she'd reeled from a sudden, persistent headache and had even vomited. Had she been more mindful of symbolism, it might be said that she now awaited a *somatic vacua*, the very *personification* of her feelings.

Only a lone passenger alighted from the bus, and it was not Wilbur.

Over a minute was required to permit of Kyler's safe descent from the bus step, but once his cane was properly planted, and his feet on the ground, he stepped forward toward Sary, dark of countenance but bizarrely fulgent of eye. At once he said, "Aye, fair gull, 'tis to the gods we be all subjected, and with every shadow they may drop afore us, there come a grace ef we be so desarvin'. Of this, I believe, ye already have a bit'a mind."

The verbiage affected Sary with confusion and even agitation. Her spirit demanded that she immediately ask where Wilbur was; however...

The words became like a mass of logs clogging a river's course.

The bus blundered away, leaving a wake of dust which, once cleared, left the black-clad soothsayer standing at Sary's other side. Finally, the portent which so darkened her psyche allowed for speech. She said bluntly, "He's dead, ain't he?"

The strange bald man did not hesitate, nor did he mince the words of his reply. "Aye, Wilbur Whateley, ye're devot'd mate, be no more'a this airth, but who's ta say this airth here be the only 'un? 'Twas a dog of a most vicious sart which spell the tall man's end—"

Sary exclaimed with some adamance: "Then where be the grace that's s'posed ta come too! With Wilbur dead, I might's wal be dead myself!"

"Nay, gull, for what ye feel be the end'a ye jess really be the stert." This was idealism and foolish rhetoric which, even if Sary knew what such words meant, she suspected at once that Kyler was only attempting to dull the blade-like pain that cut into her. No condolence could appease her now, nor any mode of rationalization. Wilbur was dead, and a reversion to her previous life was the only substitute. She would resort to self-annihilation before allowing such a consequence. No more intercourse for money, no more penises in her mouth. No more ingesting semen, laving horrific anuses with her tongue, or submitting to any further manner of carnal degradation.

No more.

"Take heart, gull," the fortune-teller offered, and into her hand he placed a sheet of paper tied in a roll. Then he began to walk away, his cane scuffing the dirt road's surface.

"What's this?" Sary demanded in a clap of a voice.

"'Tis Wilbur's legacy, thet is. And ye're new life."

"What?" she bellowed at the departing figure, but each time she blinked, the lame man's progress away from her seemed to double in an impossible amount of time. Indeed, he appeared to have traversed a mile in just minutes.

Crushed, outraged, and forlorn, Sary looked at the roll in her hand, then trod in her shiny black garment back to the tool-house. It was here she sat for hours, her eyes blank upon the old wooden walls. Certainly, the roll would prove a letter from Wilbur to her which, no matter how affectionate, she could not bear to read. A final letter was nothing but the inscription upon a grave-stone. Sary did not want to be reminded that she'd never see Wilbur again, for the missive would only *verify* that and, hence, distill her misery. She even considered killing herself without ever opening the note but...

Some unknown force countermanded the notion.

Not till sundown did Sary rise from her glum seat on the cot. She struck flint and steel, lit the lamp, then arranged herself at Wilbur's great desk. Some minutes more were expended before she untied the tube of paper.

One sheet was all she expected; what she found instead were several, the top three of which contained unintelligible scrawl arranged in numbered passages, seven in all. The writing seemed different from that of the various sheets

173

she'd seen on his desk. No, this scrawl was penned with a seemingly greater care, as if to afford her a sharper possibility of interpretation; while the strange words were interspersed often with hyphens. She scanned a random line: *6) Guh-narl-ebb, eye shub- negg add-uk zynn nem-blud nie-ar-lat-hotep.*

Sary maintained a glum stare at the sheets. What possible reason could exist for having the bald man deliver to her such bizarre lines of writing?

The fourth and fifth sheet appeared as she'd expected: lines she could read, and tightly composed as if their author we heeding space. Sary steeled herself, then began to read:

Deer Sary: I writ this ahead uv time in case things turn out less'n the way I wud prefer, which means if yew be reading this, I be dead. I take Kyler to the collige with me so's I'd have someone to bring back this message in case I got hurt or kilt. By now, especially after using the Voorish ta see my brother, ye know well I am not from hereabouts. My father come from a place far off from the Earth, way on up in the stars. It all be part of a plan that is importint, and of which ye be a strong part if ye chooze.

First thing I got to tell you mite not like but I hope yew do. I warn't speakin no lies when I tell yew severul days past that you need not wurry bout gettin pregnant by me on account my seed not be compatible with yor womb. This be true, but, well, it all change after lass night when you went to the winder that them men busted out and then got ye reel close to my brother. See, theres things in my brothers skin and breth that when he get too close to someone hereabout WORK INTA that personz blood and change em, and what it done was it change YOU, it change yer WOMB so's my seed become whut's called POTENT.

This means, Sary, you be pregnant this very second, pregnant from our lovemakin. Hope ye dont be mad, but it just be the way it is. Tis whut the gods want. It be best that we foller what they want cuz they know what is best for us. Acorse if this don't be to your liking, tis yore right ta git a abortion which is what that man ye know Doc Houghton know how to do.

I hope ye do not do this thogh, on account uv what be in

*yew now is somethin we make together, and be a expreshion
of how I feel for ye.*

Sary may have stared at the passage for a solid hour, but
from the second after she'd read the passage, her misery had
been banished, to be refilled by a joy which felt brighter than
the sun. Now she knew the root of this morning's unbidden
headache and bout of vomiting—*morning* sickness.

I'm gonna have a baby! WILBUR'S baby!

When she regained control of her emotions, she read on:

*What ye need to know rite off is I'm leevin all the Whateley
gold to ye. It'll provide for you always and make it so ye
never have to get with fellas again for money. It be hid in
the liddle fenced cemetary out back, under the slab marked
Silas Ephriam Whateley. Ye'll need a pry bar to git up the
slab and a rope ta slide it back and fourth on account it is
very heavy, but what ya got to do ferst is cover the wood plank
hangin on the nearest ash tree. It got things wrote on it that
make all who look in the grave see nothing but a skeletin,
however that coffin really be fulla gold. It's like a spell, called
a Imperceptibility Conjuration.*

Sary could not conceive of such an endowment. Her
destitution had changed to incredible affluence in a single
moment...

*What also be hid in the coffin is a metal box what got in
it all the most valuble pages from the books I got in the shed,
mostly from the hinged book but also from other books. The
payges was all copied by me so to keep em safe. Soon ye will
need to start readin these pages so's to lern em. Lotta things in
those pages that'll give ye powers like ye never dreemed, and
I mean MAGICK powers.*

Of this, Sary could scarcely maintain her equanimity. Was
Wilbur crazy to say such things? Was there *really* such a thing
as magic?

Then she recollected the Voorish Sign, and what she'd seen...

Of course there was magic!

And now it seemed that Wilbur had bestowed it unto her...

My darling, if ye choose to be a part uv all this I am talkin bout, then first chance ye get, you take the biggest chunk of gold in Great Uncle Silas' grave, which be werth a thousand dollars eezy, and ye give it to Prudence Naller so to buy her big fancy barn which be up four sale now. Ye need that barn on account it will be big enough for all ye need. Don't mention none to Prudence Naller bout how ye know me, just give her that bloon of gold and that ole fussbudget will be happy to sell ye the barn.

The information, of course, left Sary rather fuddled. A barn? Why would Wilbur want her to buy a barn, when his own livestock was barely existent now?

Buy the barn tomorow, then move right in, on account ye gotta get out of that tool shed an away from my house soon. My brother is fixing to bust quarters shortly and ye can't be anyweer near him when that happenz. Move all ye need from the shed to the barn but leave the big book with hinges and other papers there. There be no need to bother with em on account all you need is already in the copies in Great Uncle Silass grave. That man I told ye about, Armitage, he know I got that big book and if it is not there after I die, he will know someone else got their hands on it. So jest leeve it. The papers I copy give ya all the power ye need for the future. Once ye read those papers in the grave, ye'll understand why you is importint, and why our BABY be importint.

At this, Sary determined herself. No, she did not understand, but she received the distinct impression that once she read the material he'd referred to, she *would*. The *baby*, now, was most crucial to her.

Ye'll understand more and more as time go on, by what ya learn from the papers and by what ye lern from even the air, once ye come into their graces...

Sary continued to stare and stare.

The rest uv the sheets that Kyler give will look amighty strange ta ye but that be becuz I translated the words from the good copy they got at Miskatonic which replace the mussed up words in mine. This be the rite way of the words from Page 751. They are chants, what ye say aloud three times apiece on the special days up on Sentinel Hill. Roodmas, the Walpurgis, Hallowe'en. See, I wrote the chants down in a manner that be called PHONETIC, which mean it allow you to READ the words the way they is supposed to SOUND.
These words uv the chants be the most importint words ever knowed in all the world.

Sary felt an excitement buzzing in her veins. Somehow, crazy as all this sounded, she knew it was true, as if there were some component of *the very air around her* which imparted conviction and trust...

Yes. The very air around her.

And there is other things on them sheets which be spells, incantations, hexes, and wards which ye'll learn how ta do. These are things thatll help ye along the way, and protect ye from bad folks and such. It is a tremendiss power ye will have, Sary. Though I be ded in body I am not in spirit. Soon ye will even be able to see me when ya do the Voorish. It will be not my ghost but what's calt my eidolon, and I'll be able to help guide ye. Don't be confused, my sweethart, just do all what I say, and ye will see! Grate things be comin!

I'll be able to see Wilbur again! her thoughts rejoiced. The same way she saw the old man, and that pale-skinned women earlier, after she'd done the sign! Wilbur would still be with her in a sense!

177

And what I need to explane now is this: that baby ye got in yer belly? It really be TWO babies, twins. One will be like me, and one like that One in the house, my brother. You will grow to love em both once ye find out what this be all about...

Twins? Sary's eyes bloomed. *One like Wilbur and one...*
Like that gigantic, tentacled monster inside the house...
Sary rubbed her belly through the diaphanous gown.
I don't matter none that it be like that thing. All that matter is it be from Wilbur...
More and more, she was beginning to understand.

One more thing, then I be off. Once all be done by us that our god need to be done, the world will change for the better, back to the way it is supost to be, and I will get a new body by means of what's called Transfiguration. Yew will too, and we will be together again. Once the earth is cleared off.
Until this time come, pleese know I love you, Sary, with all my hart, and I always will. Forever.

Love,
Wilbur

Yes.
Once the earth is cleared off.
Sary learned quickly, from the papers in the metal box in Silas Whateley's grave, and from the density of the air in special places where the Words had been uttered, and from the muttering underneath the ground at Special Times.
And from Wilbur's momentary presences when she made the Voorish.
She had bought the Naller barn the very next day, just as Wilbur had posthumously requested. It was a great spacious barn, well large enough for what she now understood would begin to occupy it after nine months had passed. It also possessed several smaller rooms for herself and the other things she'd brought along. She read and re-read every day now, and would continue to, and would practice all the things

she was learning constantly. Wilbur's death had given Sary a *new* life to live while not merely waiting for the time she would be with him again, but also to be a fine, resplendent mother for the two children she would soon give birth to. This she knew, for all she was worth.

She knew something else as well.

When she did indeed give birth to the twins, she would name the human baby Wilbur.

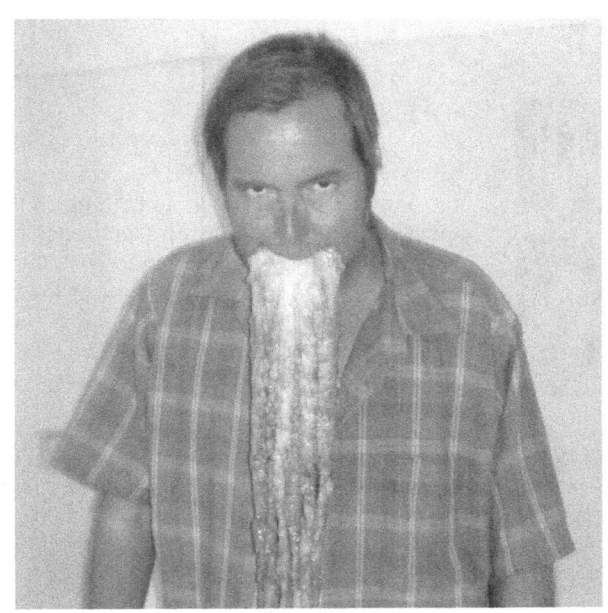

ABOUT THE AUTHOR

Edward Lee has authored close to 50 books in the field of horror; he specializes in hardcore fare. His most recent novels are LUCIFER'S LOTTERY and the Lovecraftian THE HAUNTER OF THE THRESHOLD. His movie HEADER was released on DVD by Synapse Film in June, 2009. Lee lives in Largo, Florida.

deadite press

"Header" Edward Lee - In the dark backwoods, where law enforcement doesn't dare tread, there exists a special type of revenge. Something so awful that it is only whispered about. Something so terrible that few believe it is real. Stewart Cummings is a government agent whose life is going to Hell. His wife is ill and to pay for her medication he turns to bootlegging. But things will get much worse when bodies begin showing up in his sleepy small town. Victims of an act known only as "a Header."

"Red Sky" Nate Southard - When a bank job goes horrifically wrong, career criminal Danny Black leads his crew from El Paso into the deserts of New Mexico in a desperate bid for escape. Danny soon finds himself with no choice but to hole up in an abandoned factory, the former home of Red Sky Manufacturing. Danny and his crew aren't the only living things in Red Sky, though. Something waits in the abandoned factory's shadows, something horrible and violent. Something hungry. And when the sun drops, it will feast.

"Zombies and Shit" Carlton Mellick III - Twenty people wake to find themselves in a boarded-up building in the middle of the zombie wasteland. They soon discover they have been chosen as contestants on a popular reality show called Zombie Survival. Each contestant is given a backpack of supplies and a unique weapon. Their goal: be the first to make it through the zombie-plagued city to the pick-up zone alive. But because there's only one seat available on the helicopter, the contestants not only have to fight against the hordes of the living dead, they must also fight each other.

"Muerte Con Carne" Shane McKenzie - Human flesh tacos, hardcore wrestling, and angry cannibal Mexicans, Welcome to the Border! Felix and Marta came to Mexico to film a documentary on illegal immigration. When Marta suddenly goes missing, Felix must find his lost love in the small border town. A dangerous place housing corrupt cops, borderline maniacs, and something much more worse than drug gangs, something to do with a strange Mexican food cart...

www.ingramcontent.com/pod-product-compliance
Lightning Source LLC
Chambersburg PA
CBHW060111260626
47160CB00005B/1856